Caught Dead-Handed . . .

He watched long enough to know Rawhide Rawlins wasn't among these men—these slaves. Slocum drifted through the buildings, hidden by heavy shadows. He found a bunkhouse filled with sleeping men and loud snores. Rawlins might be here. He started to lift the latch and enter when he heard the metallic click of a rifle being cocked behind him.

"You're a dead man if you so much as twitch toward that gun of yours," came the cold command. "Get those hands up and turn around."

Slocum did as he was told and saw he was in a worse predicament than he'd thought. Not one guard but three had caught him. He might throw down on one and hope to escape, but three? No way in hell was he going to shoot his way out of this.

JAKE LOGAN

SLOCUM
AND THE
THUNDERBIRD

JOVE BOOKS, NEW YORK

THE BERKLEY PUBLISHING GROUP
Published by the Penguin Group
Penguin Group (USA)
375 Hudson Street, New York, New York 10014, USA

USA | Canada | UK | Ireland | Australia | New Zealand | India | South Africa | China

Penguin Books Ltd., Registered Offices: 80 Strand, London WC2R 0RL, England
For more information about the Penguin Group, visit penguin.com.

SLOCUM AND THE THUNDERBIRD

A Jove Book / published by arrangement with the author

Jove Books are published by The Berkley Publishing Group.
JOVE® is a registered trademark of Penguin Group (USA).
The "J" design is a trademark of Penguin Group (USA).

For information, address: The Berkley Publishing Group,
a division of Penguin Group (USA),
375 Hudson Street, New York, New York 10014.

ISBN: 978-0-515-15384-2

PUBLISHING HISTORY
Jove mass-market edition / October 2013

PRINTED IN THE UNITED STATES OF AMERICA

10 9 8 7 6 5 4 3 2 1

Cover illustration by Sergio Giovine.

ALWAYS LEARNING   **PEARSON**

1

One instant John Slocum sat astride the strawberry roan, the next he was sailing through the air. He landed hard in the corral and rolled into a tight ball to avoid flashing hooves lashing out at his head.

"Dang, Slocum, that horse shore do hate your guts," called Rawhide Rawlins from the safety of the top rail.

"Get him outta there, you buffoon," cried Lee Dupree, acting while Rawlins didn't budge.

Dupree took off his floppy-brimmed hat and waved it to get the bronco's attention. Nostrils flaring and paws still slicing through the air just above Slocum's head, the horse wasn't going to be deterred. Slocum realized this when Dupree couldn't divert the cayuse's attention. He rolled fast just as the horse dropped its hooves where his head had been a split second earlier. Slocum kept rolling until he was under the bottom corral rail and away from the unbroken horse.

"Gotta give you credit, Slocum," Rawlins said. "Ain't nobody could stay on that outlaw's back as long as you just did."

Slocum dusted himself off and warily climbed to the rail

to sit beside the cowboy. Dupree got the horse turning hard, then reversed his direction and ducked out of the corral to join his partners.

"Rawhide ain't right 'bout many things, but this one he surely is," Dupree said. "No disgrace getting tossed off this one in the wink of an eye. He's about the worst bucker I ever did see."

Slocum studied the horse. After the Box M cattle had been driven to the railhead, he had turned his attention to the stock remaining. That included this varmint. The Box M foreman had lassoed the wild stallion a couple months earlier, but this was Slocum's first try at breaking it. The way he ached from the fall, he wasn't sure he'd be up to another attempt anytime soon. The trail drive had tuckered him out, down with the flu as he had been, but giving up had never been a part of his disposition. The Box M had fallen on hard times and the drive had been done with a dozen fewer cowboys than usual, so he couldn't rightly let the owner down.

George Holman had gotten top dollar for the beeves, and a bonus was likely coming as a result. Slocum thought that was only fair. He, Rawlins, Dupree, and the other drovers had done double the work. A bonus would suit them all just fine.

"Hey, Slocum, you two, boss wants you in the main house right now!"

Slocum didn't cotton much to the foreman, but Lucas Underwood knew his business. What galled Slocum was how much of a skinflint he was. Food on the trail kept a cowpuncher happy. Underwood had fired the cook, who had been the only man who could spin a yarn good enough around the campfire to make the rest of the cowboys forget their sorry plight.

But that was all changed. Slocum knew Holman was rolling in the money. Next year would be even better. Underwood might even hire back the yarn-spinning cook.

That passing thought made him pause. Next year? He

drifted from one job to another, and here he was thinking about working for the same rancher a second season. The Box M was safely on the western side of the Wall cutting through South Dakota and right at the edge of the Badlands. This was terrible country, fierce and wild and beautiful. Slocum had taken a liking to it. Given a good job, he'd stay another year.

Eyeing Underwood waving all high and mighty at them put thoughts of taking the man's job as foreman into Slocum's head. There wasn't much about a cattle ranch that Slocum didn't know. He had ideas for more than a few changes that would put even more money in Holman's pocket, given the chance to try them.

"Get your asses over here *now*."

"What's so all-fired important?" Rawhide Rawlins kicked free of the rail and dropped heavily. He hitched up his jeans, emphasizing his bowed legs and showing the sides of his battered boots. "Cain't you just let us do some relaxin'?"

"That's not what I'd say Slocum was doin'," Dupree said. "Another few minutes and you'd've broke that stallion."

"Told you not to go botherin' the horse," Underwood said.

"Well, you ain't gonna break it for your own," Dupree said. "You can't hardly sit astride that docile mare you ride without fallin' off at a trot."

Slocum saw something in the foreman's expression that his two friends missed. Such a jibe ought to have turned Underwood livid. It didn't. A small smile curled the corners of his mouth.

"Y'all come along."

"Reckon we can do that," Rawlins said. "Not like we got more important things to do now that we got the herd to market and all sold."

Slocum walked silently while Dupree and Rawlins chattered like magpies. He kept his eye on Underwood. The foreman walked about as fast as he ever had, showing he was heading toward something that pleased him. Slocum was even warier when they went into the ranch house and saw George Holman rocked back in his chair behind a huge cherrywood desk.

"Took you long enough to get them in here," Holman said.

Slocum and the others spotted the large pile of greenbacks on the desk. That was more than they'd likely make in ten years of cow punching. Slocum didn't miss how Holman followed their gaze and hastily swept the money from the desk into a burlap bag.

"Underwood's told me what you three have been up to," the rancher said.

"Yup, it's true," Dupree said, grinning.

"You admit it?" Holman's eyes widened in surprise, then narrowed. His lips thinned to a razor slash. "Then you know what I'm going to say."

"A big bonus, that's for certain sure," Rawlins said.

"What?"

Slocum watched the byplay between the men and moved his hand toward his left hip. He didn't pack his iron when working. His Colt Navy rested in its holster amid his gear back in the bunkhouse. Rawlins and Dupree were saying one thing and Holman something entirely different. He felt a knot forming in his gut.

"Slocum here ain't busted that bronc yet, but he will. And the three of us, we worked like ten men on the drive. How big's our bonus?" Rawlins smiled so much his mustache tips twitched about like they had come alive.

"You're thieves. The lot of you! You stole fifty head of cattle and sold them on your own."

"How do you figure that?" Slocum asked. He didn't look at the rancher but at the foreman. "We lost about that many head on the drive, and that's a mighty small number for such a large herd."

"You rustled them beeves!" Holman slammed his fists

down on the desk and half stood. He leaned forward. "I ought to string you up, the three of you. Underwood's more merciful. He convinced me to just send you on your way."

"We worked all season long," said Slocum. "We didn't steal any of your cattle. Cheat us out of a bonus if that's your style, but you owe us for the work we did over the last six months."

"Get out of my sight! Get out or I'll horsewhip you, you rustlers!"

Slocum heard the soft hiss of gunmetal across leather. He swung around and stared down the bore of Underwood's .44. From the expression on his face, Underwood wanted an excuse to pull the trigger.

"You cain't do this! We worked. Hard," protested Dupree.

"You stole from me."

"What's your proof?" Slocum asked. He kept his green eyes fixed on Underwood.

"He saw you with the cattle. Him and two others as they rode in. You got to town first, and you had already cut them from the main herd."

"Johnson and Pig-eye," Slocum said, naming two of Underwood's cronies. "You're taking their word over ours?"

"Damned right I am. Underwood's worked for me these last four years, worked harder than any man I ever saw."

"'Cept us," cut in Dupree.

"He's honest. If he and the other two say you stole fifty head, I'm not calling them liars."

"I am, Mr. Holman," Slocum said. "They—"

That was as far as he got. He half turned back to the rancher and caught the blur of the six-gun swinging toward his head. Sudden pain blossomed and he went to his knees. He heard shouts and then a gunshot. Try as he might, he couldn't get his legs under him. He tried to stand, but his knees had turned to water.

In the far distance, through the blackness and a roaring in his ears, he heard horses and loud voices.

* * *

"Never thought you'd come around, Slocum," Rawlins said. "You got a lump the size of my fist on the side of your head."

Slocum touched the aching, throbbing knot and winced. Rawlins had a way of exaggerating. This time he spoke the truth. Slocum traced around the bump put there when Underwood buffaloed him. That returning memory caused Slocum to sit up so fast that dizziness hit him, then a cold anger that wasn't to be denied settled over him.

"Whoa, Slocum, you set yerself back," Dupree said.

Slocum shoved the man's hand off his shoulder. He tried to stand but had to settle for just looking around. His vision cleared.

"Where the hell are we?" he asked.

"Underwood and those mangy dog-eater partners of his got the drop on us after he laid his six-gun up alongside your head. Mr. Holman ordered us off the Box M."

"They threw our gear in the back of a wagon, drove us out here a ways, and dumped us."

"They stole our horses?"

"Looks like," Rawlins said. "My old mare's so broke down, feedin' her's gonna be a burden on them, but I do miss her."

Slocum got to his feet and took a couple shaky steps. Anger stiffened his back and knees. He bent and pulled out his Colt still stuffed into its cross-draw holster. Two quick movements lashed it around his waist and settled down on his hip.

"You always had the look of a shootist, Slocum, no matter how good you was at punching them cows. You know how to use that smoke wagon, don't you?" Dupree sounded a trifle uneasy. "What you fixin' to do?"

"First thing is to get our horses. Underwood might have framed us for rustling, but horse thievery is worse." He swung his saddle over his shoulder, got his bearings, and started walking back up the road toward the Box M.

"You thinkin' on shootin' any of them, Slocum?" Rawhide Rawlins hitched up his drawers, then swung his saddle to his shoulder.

Slocum looked at him.

"If I need to."

"Count me in, then," Rawlins said. "Ain't nobody steals from me."

"Me, too," Les Dupree said, joining the other two. "'Fore I shoot anybody, I need a six-shooter."

"That won't be a problem, not when I'm done," Slocum said.

The three of them hiked a couple miles before Slocum pointed to a ravine that ran across the Box M.

"We won't be seen until we're almost at the barn," he said. "Then we go retrieve our horses."

"And then we shoot 'em up?" Dupree sounded leery of such bloodshed.

"Ain't Holman's fault, not much at least, since he believed his foreman," Rawlins said.

"He went along." Dupree's bitterness set the tone for the rest of the argument.

The two slowly talked themselves into the mood Slocum had endured the entire way back onto the ranch. Underwood might have lied, but it hadn't taken much to convince Holman. That pile of greenbacks showed his interest, and it wasn't in the truth.

"Anybody in sight?" Slocum asked. He dropped his gear and pulled down the brim of his hat to shield his eyes against the afternoon sun as he peered over the ravine bank.

"Looks like Holman and Underwood over on the ranch house porch," said Rawlins. He popped up again, then dropped like a prairie dog worried over a pack of wolves. "Holman's clutchin' a bag to his chest like it has his heart inside."

Slocum slid the leather thong off his Colt's hammer, scrambled up the bank, and walked to the barn, while the other two argued over what to do. They weren't armed. He was. Ignoring the ranch owner and foreman, he walked into the barn. A black gelding in the first stall jerked its head around and neighed at seeing him.

"You'll be out of here soon enough," Slocum said, patting the horse's neck. He found a bucket of oats and put some in the trough in front of the horse. Grazing out on the sparse Dakota plains meant less to eat in the very near future.

He found the other men's mounts and fed and watered them, too, before he rummaged about in the small tack room. Two old Henry rifles and boxes of ammo caught his eye. He stacked them just outside the door while he poked about, hunting for anything else. A Damascus barreled shotgun looked like it would blow up in the hands of whoever fired it next. He left it.

Soft sounds at the barn door caused him to grab for his Colt Navy. He relaxed when he saw Rawlins and Dupree. They lugged not only their own saddles but his as well.

"Figgered you'd prefer to ride on a saddle than bareback," Rawlins said. He saw his mare contentedly chewing away and nodded. "Thankee kindly fer feedin' that tired old bag o' bones."

"Here," Slocum said, tossing the rifles to the men. He gave them the boxes of ammunition and waited as they loaded and checked the actions. Only when he was sure they were loaded for bear did he ask, "Where'd Holman and Underwood get off to? Heard hoofbeats."

"Well, it's like this, Slocum," Rawlins said. "I overheard Holman sayin' they was ridin' into town to stash that wad of greenbacks in the bank."

"That's *our* money," Dupree said. "No difference 'n them stealin' it at gunpoint."

Slocum touched the side of his head. They *had* stolen the money at gunpoint.

"Let's go after them two and talk some sense into them." He touched the ebony handle of his six-shooter, then dropped his hand away when he saw the men staring hard at him.

Both looked a tad frightened, but he couldn't expect more from them. They'd been cowboys all their lives. Any gun-handling they'd done was likely only shooting varmints, some hunting, and taking potshots at old tin cans set on fence posts.

He said nothing more, saddled, and led his gelding out into the warm autumn sun. Easily mounting, he started after the rancher.

"Slocum, hold up. They got a head start on us. If we cut across country, we kin overtake them 'fore they reach town." Dupree pointed off at an angle from the road.

He didn't bother answering. Slocum simply turned his gelding's head and trotted away. Dupree knew the land in that direction better than he did. It took a half hour before they encountered a deep ravine that made further progress a problem.

Slocum seethed at the delay as they rode the bank until they found a way down into the arroyo, then worked another fifteen minutes until a break in the tall bank afforded them a return to level ground. Without a word, Slocum set a faster pace than either of the others' horses could maintain. Even then, too much time had been wasted.

He rode down Halliday's main street, then drew rein and watched as Holman left the bank empty-handed. The rancher had deposited his ill-gotten money in the secure vault.

"Whew, Slocum, you surely did git here in jig time." Rawlins saw his former boss mount and ride away. Holman didn't see them. "Does that mean what I think it does?"

"He put the money in the bank," Slocum said.

"What're we gonna do now?" Dupree asked.

Both Slocum and Rawlins turned toward him, but to Slocum's surprise, Rawhide gave the only answer to their problem.

"We rob the bank."

Then both of them stared at him. Slocum was the only one with experience using a six-shooter—and robbing a bank.

2

"Good idea," muttered Slocum.

"Yeah, they owe us," said Dupree, obviously trying to convince himself.

Then both men stared at Slocum and, as one, asked, "How do we do it?"

The two of them laughed nervously before Rawlins went on. "We ain't bank robbers. I heard tell of men robbin' banks and trains, but I never seen it done with my own eyes."

Slocum paid no attention to the men. He carefully studied the streets of Halliday, taking note of how sleepy-looking the town was. This late in the afternoon, men hadn't come in from the ranches yet to whoop it up in one of the half-dozen saloons lining the main street. The marshal's office at the far end of the street might have been deserted for all the activity there. No horse tethered outside, men didn't head for the jailhouse on business. If anything, they veered away from it.

Slocum considered what that might mean. He had come into town more than once to get drunk and find himself a woman, but he'd never seen the marshal. Not raising a big enough ruckus might be part of it, but Slocum thought enforcement was lax in this town. The ranchers preferred it that way and would call Marshal Hillstrom on the carpet if he threw too many of their hands into jail for whooping it up. That said nothing about how fired up the marshal might get if the bank with all the ranchers' money in it was robbed.

"How do we plan it? I mean, what do we need to do?" Rawlins asked. "'Fore we stick it up."

"Pull up your bandannas like this," Slocum said, tugging at his sweaty neck scarf and tying it over the bridge of his nose so only his eyes peered out from under his hat brim.

"We can do that," Dupree said, duplicating Slocum's effort. "Then we—"

"Then you take out those rifles I gave you and chamber a round." Slocum kicked free of his horse, looped the reins around an iron ring mounted at the side of the bank, drew his six-shooter, and went to the front door. "Follow me," he said.

With a quick kick, he slammed open the double doors so hard they smashed against the inside walls. Glass in one shattered, sounding like a gunshot. This got all the tellers' attention.

Slocum stepped inside and heard the broken glass grinding under his boots. He lifted his pistol and aimed it squarely at the bank president at his desk behind a low railing to the left.

"This is a robbery. Keep your hands where I can see them or *he* gets ventilated." To emphasize his order, Slocum cocked the Colt. In the small bank lobby it sounded like the peal of doom.

"Grab the money," Rawlins said excitedly. "We take all of it, Slo—"

"Only what's ours," Slocum said, cutting the man off before he could blurt out the name. Louder, he said, "Where's Holman's bag? The one he just came in with?"

The teller closest to the bank president held up the burlap bag.

Dupree snatched it from the man's shaking hand.

"We kin get more," he said, half fearfully, half in greed.

"Is it all there?"

"Cain't tell," Dupree said, peering into the bag.

"Empty your cash drawer," Slocum ordered the teller. "Just to be sure."

"You can't do this," the president said, half standing. His florid face turned beet red when Slocum planted a bullet into the fancy desk smack in front of him. Wood splinters flew into his face.

"We're only taking some of it."

"Got it," Dupree said, holding up the stuffed bag.

Slocum backed away as Rawlins and Dupree left ahead of him, cackling like hens at how easy the robbery had been. When he was sure they had mounted, he pulled the doors shut behind him and vaulted into the saddle. As he put his heels to the gelding's flanks, he saw the bank president poke his fiery red face through the broken window. Slocum sagged inside when the man fired a hideout pistol. A derringer wouldn't do a whole lot of damage at such a distance, but Slocum couldn't count on the heavy slug not finding its way into his horse.

Slocum began firing, slowly, methodically. The banker's bald head disappeared, amid cries of confusion. The tellers had crowded close behind and the retreating bank officer had collided with them. That suited Slocum just fine. The more confusion he created inside the bank, the less likely any of them were to give a decent description.

Galloping after the other two, Slocum knew the telling of the robbery would grow the longer it took for the marshal to show up. Even now, the bank employees might be willing to swear that a dozen men had stuck them up and give descriptions that would fit no one in the entire territory.

"Slow down, or you'll kill the horses," Slocum called as

they rode around a bend in the road and got out of sight of town.

"We done it. Jist as slick as snot, we done it!" chortled Dupree.

"We'll ride a ways farther, divvy it up, and then go our separate ways," Slocum said. Due west rose wind-eroded mountains that hid the worst of the Badlands. Out here it was hilly, but there a man could get lost mighty fast.

Get lost—or lose a posse.

"Split up?" Rawlins asked, confused. "We're partners. We kin—"

"We split the loot, then go different ways. If you two want to rendezvous later, make your plans now before we stop."

"You don't want to ride with us, Slocum?" Dupree sounded hurt.

"We've got to make it as hard as we can for the law to find us."

"Sounds like you've got some experience in that department," Rawlins said.

Slocum cut off the road that angled southwest toward the town of Overton and trotted straight west for what appeared to be a pass leading deeper into the Badlands. He had more than his share of experience dodging the law. Although he had never poked through the stack of wanted posters in the Halliday marshal's office, he likely would find an old reward on his head. After the war he had returned to Slocum's Stand in Calhoun, Georgia, only to find a carpetbagger judge had taken a shine to the land and intended to raise Tennessee walkers.

A faked tax lien was all it took for the judge and his hired gun to ride out to seize the property. He had gotten more land—and less—than he'd bargained for. Slocum had buried the two down by the springhouse, then had ridden away. Killing a federal judge, even a thieving carpetbagger judge, was a crime Reconstruction bureaucrats looked poorly on. The wanted poster had dogged his tracks ever since—

not that he hadn't accumulated a few more along the way. Working for a living never bothered him, but sometimes using a six-gun and a mask, as he just had, was the only way to keep body and soul together.

More than this, it often dealt out justice where the law refused to budge. The town marshal would never have listened to Slocum and the others' pleas that they had been robbed of their horses and salaries. The Box M spread was about the largest in the county. Holman was respected, and even if his reputation included rooking hardworking cowboys out of their due, the marshal wouldn't have listened. A judge wouldn't listen and no one in Halliday was likely to either. The Box M brought too much business to town to risk angering the owner.

"Might be you don't think much of us as partners," Dupree said.

"You said it yourself. I've got experience robbing banks. You don't. This doesn't have anything to do with how good a partner you are on the trail," he explained, trying not to let an edge of anger cut along with his words. "We've got to play it smart."

"Hell, they won't come for us," Dupree said. "Marshal Hillstrom's not budged from town in months."

Slocum brought his horse to a halt and put his finger to his lips to quiet the other two. He cocked his head to one side, then turned slowly so he located the shouts. From what few words he could make out as the anger drifted on the cool afternoon breeze, several men were riled up over the bank robbery. They had mistakenly thought the robbers had remained on the road that curved around and headed to the southwest.

"Either of you know how good a tracker Hillstrom is?"

Dupree and Rawlins exchanged looks, then shrugged.

"Heard tell he used to be an Army scout for the Seventh 'fore he got his leg all busted up. Might jist be a tall tale."

Slocum couldn't risk that it wasn't. The posse would

follow the road until the marshal found a rise that let him look a mile or two ahead. Not seeing his quarry, he would backtrack and hunt for any spot the trio might have left the road. Slocum cursed under his breath. Not doing anything to hide their tracks, at least for a short distance, might be their undoing.

"It's too late to cover our hoofprints," he said. "We ride as fast as we can for the hills and lose ourselves there."

"Does get rocky mighty fast. They don't call these Badlands fer nuthin'," Dupree said.

"You reckon the hard ground'll confuse the posse?" Rawlins kept looking over his shoulder into the twilight, as if he felt the marshal's hot breath on his neck.

"Can't hurt," Slocum said. They were reaching the end of their rope. Their horses had stumbled for more than a mile, a sure sign that they'd be on foot if they pushed too much harder. "Let's take a rest here," he finally said, not wanting to but realizing the need.

"Good thing. Poor ole Betsy's staggerin' around like she's drunk," Rawlins said.

"Like you, the last time we went to town," Dupree teased him.

Slocum walked his horse around to cool it down a mite, then began a hunt for water. They needed more than the few drops remaining in their canteens, the horses most of all.

He skirted a rock, then stopped dead in his tracks. Only gathering shadows as the sun sank behind the hills before them saved his hide. Not twenty feet away, two Sioux braves watered their horses at a small spring bubbling up into a rock basin. Moving slowly, Slocum stepped back. He made certain each foot was secure before putting weight down. To turn a stone now would alert the Indians. While they were partially hidden in the same shadows that had saved him, he caught the glint of faint light off war paint on their faces.

When he pressed his back against the rock, he dared not

breathe again until he felt secure enough to get the hell away. Walking faster now, he found the two cowboys arguing over some picayune thing.

"We got company. Hush! Keep your voices low. There are two Sioux warriors on the other side of this rock."

"What'll we do, Slocum? Should we cut 'em down?" Rawlins clutched his rifle so hard that his hands shook.

"Let 'em water their horses, then go their way. When it's safe, we'll water our horses from the same pool."

"But a war party! Them's dangerous souls, Slocum. The Sioux been hankerin' fer a fight nigh on three months," said Rawlins.

"Rawhide's right, fer a change. They don't like the white man diggin' up their land for gold."

Slocum quieted the two. They both stewed in their own juices. When they were about ready to pop from the strain of not arguing, he motioned them to follow. It had been the better part of a half hour. The Sioux braves should have finished watering their mounts and gone on their way.

He let out a pent-up breath when he saw he was right. Darkness had fallen, making it difficult to see. The moon wouldn't be up for another hour to light their trail. If he remembered rightly, it was three-quarters waxing full and, clouds willing, would give them light enough to ride deeper into the Badlands.

"Fill your canteens, too," Slocum ordered. "We don't know when the next watering hole will spring up in front of us. Either of you come this way before?" He didn't have to see them shaking their heads in the dark to know they all rode blindly into terrain that swallowed up unwary riders without a trace.

Retreating was out of the question. That would put them into the arms of the law from Halliday. Slocum had the feeling in his gut that the marshal wasn't the kind to give up easily. Not finding the bank robbers on the road would only incense him.

"Scary ridin' after dark like this," Dupree said.

"Give your horse her head," Slocum advised. "She'll do better than you can in the dark."

"Ain't never knowed a horse that could see in the dark like an owl." Dupree craned his neck around and added, "Night's so dark the bats'll stay home."

"Moonrise in an hour," Rawlins said with confidence.

Slocum let the two ride ahead as he brought up the rear to keep a sharp lookout. Less than a half hour later, he was glad he had not let either of them watch their back trail. The sound of ponies alerted him to the Indians coming after them.

He considered falling back farther, then ambushing the war party. When he caught sight of the leading two riders, he smiled. He could take care of two warriors. Then his confidence faded when he saw dark shadows crowding close behind the leading riders. He stopped counting when he reached ten.

Urging his horse to greater speed, he overtook Rawlins and Dupree at the mouth of a canyon.

"We got big trouble," he told them. "Those were only scouts back at the watering hole."

"Scouts?" Rawlins said uneasily. "You see a big war party?"

"We're not going to fight them. Outrunning them is our only chance."

Slocum looked around. A canyon angled off to their right. The one stretching ahead looked more promising since it took a sharp turn to the left only a hundred yards in. A quick look at the canyon rims warned him they had no chance in hell of finding a trail and getting out of the winding maze of rocky walls.

"Fast. Don't worry about being quiet," Slocum said. He caught the rattle of unshod hooves against rock behind them. "If we have to find a place to make a stand, I want it in a canyon where the Sioux can't flank us."

"You got the sound of a military man 'bout you, Slocum," said Rawlins. "Seems like there's a whale of a lot about you we ain't heard yet."

He had no time to relate his experiences with the CSA as a captain, even if he had anything there to brag on during his service. Slocum led them in deeper, took the sharp bend, and immediately began hunting for a spot to ambush the Indians. Outrunning them wasn't going to work. And he knew outfighting them wasn't likely any better a plan, but he wanted to die fighting rather than allowing himself to be taken captive. A war party might decide to torture their prisoners.

"Slocum," Rawlins said fearfully. "This here canyon don't go no farther. It's a box we rode into."

The moon poked up enough to cast a bright silver spotlight on the canyon mouth and beyond. He didn't have to be a frontier scout to see that Rawhide was right. He pulled his Winchester from the saddle sheath. With the Henrys he had given the other men, they could stop one good attack or maybe two halfhearted ones. During a skirmish in the dark, their accuracy wouldn't be worth shit. Worse, the muzzle flashes would be beacons in the night for the Sioux.

"Into those rocks," Slocum said. He guided the two cowboys to the best possible positions. "Take a box of ammo with you."

"Been good knowin' you, Slocum. Wish we'd had time to buy a bottle or two of whiskey with what we took from the bank."

Slocum couldn't tell who spoke because his full attention was focused on the canyon mouth. Keeping the Sioux from surrounding them was the only good thing about this otherwise indefensible position. One all-out attack would overwhelm them.

He rested his rifle on the top of a rock and leaned forward. The rough surface scraped his chest as he worked the lever, then he put his elbows down to steady the Winchester.

Dark shapes bobbed up and down on the back trail. He stopped counting when he reached eight Sioux. There wasn't any doubt the Indians had tracked them since they likely knew this stretch of the Badlands better than any white man. The canyon was a death trap.

Slocum tensed. A deadly plug drove into that rocky canyon neck as a full dozen braves sat astride their ponies, faces hidden in deep shadow as the bright moon lit them from behind. Slocum eased back on the trigger. The rifle bucked. His shot went wide but caused the Sioux to let out whoops and sight in on him. Moving to a different position to continue the attack was out of the question when the Indians began firing. The night sky was soon filled with orange lances of flame from a dozen rifles. When his rifle jammed, Slocum tossed it aside and drew his six-shooter.

"Here they come," Dupree said. He started firing wildly. Rawlins joined in.

Slocum doubted either of them came close to hitting anything, but it might not matter. If the Indians dismounted and advanced on foot, they would simply vanish into the terrain. Better that the Sioux stayed on horseback.

The war cries rang in his ears as the Indians attacked.

He knew they were goners . . . until the Indians let out a screech of fear rather than attack. All the Sioux wheeled their horses about and hightailed it away. For several seconds, Slocum couldn't believe his eyes. He finally stood and stared after the retreating riders.

The eerie shriek that ripped through the canyon caused Slocum to whirl about. He looked up and saw a bird with ten-foot outstretched wings on the canyon rim illuminated in the bright moonlight. A shiver went up his spine. He had never seen any bird that big in his life.

3

"Kill it, kill it!" Lee Dupree spun about and began firing wildly at the bird until his rifle barrel glowed a dull red. Only when the magazine came up empty did he stop, and then in his panic he worked the cocking lever mindlessly.

Slocum reached out and jerked the man's arm to spin him around. Dupree's eyes were wide with fear, and a touch of drool dribbled down his chin.

"Stop it," Slocum ordered harshly.

Only when Dupree began babbling and dropped the rifle did Slocum look up at the canyon rim. For the briefest instant he saw the dark figure and struggled to make out what it was. Then it disappeared. With the huge bird went its shrill screeches. The canyon had become so quiet that it hurt Slocum's ears. Straining, he tried to catch any sounds of rabbits running for their burrows or a hunting coyote prowling for dinner. Nothing. Even the wind had died down, turning the slot canyon into a furnace. Sunlight from the autumn day had warmed the colorful layers of rock, and they now released their stored heat, making the silence even more oppressive.

"What the hell was that?" Rawhide Rawlins said, breaking the stillness with the question Slocum had not put into words.

"Never saw anything like it," Slocum said.

"It . . . it was a thunderbird! One of them Indian spirits."

"Stop talkin' crazy, Dupree," Rawlins said uneasily. He looked at Slocum for reassurance. "There ain't no sich critter, right, Slocum?"

"We're in a box canyon. If the Sioux decide to come back, we'll be in worse shape than before."

He kicked at an empty ammo box. They were running low on cartridges, and in their current condition, after seeing the creature on the canyon rim, he doubted Dupree would put up much of a fight. Rawhide wasn't as shaken, but any hesitation would spell their deaths.

"You ain't gettin' no argument from me on that, Slocum," Dupree said. He ran to his horse. Slocum bent over and grabbed the man's discarded rifle, then tossed it to him. "Thanks," Dupree said sheepishly. Then he looked at the nighttime sky and got frightened all over again.

Slocum and Rawlins followed at a distance until they reached the canyon mouth. Slocum called for Dupree to stop while he thought on where to run. Going back into the box canyon was out of the question. Retracing their path to this point might stick their necks into a noose if Marshal Hillstrom had gotten onto their trail. Even if the lawman hadn't twigged to them leaving the main road, going in that direction would put them behind the Sioux war party.

"There," Slocum said. "You have any idea where that canyon leads?" He pointed to a dark opening in the wall of Badlands mountains.

"Don't look like it's a box, not like the other," Rawlins said. "There're a couple trails going in."

"Game trails?" Slocum trotted toward the canyon and tried to see what Rawlins had. He had to scratch his head.

There might be a trail or two here, but that didn't mean this wasn't a dead end, too. Still, the tracks looked well traveled. Another town hidden away in the hills promised safety from the Indians, if not from Halliday's marshal.

There wasn't anywhere else to flee.

He started in, following one of the faint dirt tracks. Dupree called out.

"What if it comes after us? The thunderbird?"

"There's no such thing," Slocum said. "That's a story the Indians tell around campfires, just like the stories Rawhide spins."

"He ain't much of a storyteller," Dupree said.

"I'll think on a story 'bout a cowboy without a lick of sense who got spooked and fired at some big bird and then claimed it was a thunderbird," Rawlins said.

"I saw it. I *saw* a thunderbird! What else could it have been? Rawhide? Slocum? Tell me what else it could have been."

"Saw something," Slocum allowed. "Don't know what it was since I didn't get a good enough look at it."

"You *heard* its huntin' cry. It was after us."

"Chased off the Sioux," Rawlins said, nodding.

The moon rose high enough to illuminate the trail they followed. Slocum wished it had remained low. Not only would it have hidden them from anyone behind, but it would have hidden his partners' faces. Dupree was still scared. Rawlins put up a good front, but Slocum saw how the man edged a tad closer to thinking like Dupree with every mention of the bird and its scream.

"Might have been a trick that fooled our eyes," Slocum said. "The moon looks bigger when it rises. Mid-sky, it looks tiny but it's still the same size."

"That's not so," Dupree said. "You can tell the moon shrinks as it rises. Look at it!"

Slocum had. When they were children, his older brother, Robert, had shown him how to measure it. Holding a stick at arm's length, Slocum had cut notches on either side of the moon as it peeked out over the horizon. Hours later, he had held the stick at the same distance and the moon still touched the notches. After he had told Robert, his brother had given him the knife used to cut the notches. He had always learned so much from his brother. Robert had convinced him that things weren't always the way they appeared and careful study revealed the truth.

He pushed down the memories. Robert had been killed during Pickett's Charge and had died a hero in the midst of a terribly wrong tactic.

"It might have been an eagle," Slocum said.

"You ever heard an iggle make a sound like that, Slocum? I never have, and I'm a damned sight older 'n you. And it was huge! Bigger 'n any iggle I ever set eyes on."

Slocum let Rawlins take up the argument, but it was obvious he was slowly coming around to believing Dupree was right.

"Damn Injun spirit, that's what it was," Dupree said. "They live in thunderstorms and come swoopin' down to earth and . . . and make sounds like the one we heard."

"No storm," Slocum pointed out. "Wish there was. It would hide our tracks and make any posse behind us think twice about staying on the trail."

"Might be better languishin' in the Halliday jail rather 'n bein' et by a screamin' mad thunderbird," Dupree said.

He warmed to his subject, engaging Rawlins in a discussion of Indian spirit creatures and how the Sioux got scared of their own totem. Somehow, the Sioux turning tail and running proved his argument—at least it did to Dupree. Slocum snapped the reins and rode farther ahead on the pretense of scouting.

The moon made for perfect riding. Not a cloud in the sky dimmed its light, and the silvery brilliance let Slocum keep a steady trot. From the condition of the trail, others had ridden this way not long back. He thought he saw fresh horse flop but never slowed to be sure, distracted by the dark openings of branching canyons. The Badlands were perfect to get lost in, with all the canyons and winding trails.

At the juncture of three canyons, he had to make a decision which trail to follow. The one to his left might turn back behind the box canyon where they had held off the Sioux war party. To his right yawned a huge canyon, while the one ahead swallowed the trail he already followed.

"Which way we gonna go, Slocum?" Rawhide drew rein beside him. "We keep on goin' straight?"

"We camp here and see how things look at daybreak," he said, coming to a decision. "My horse is about ready to collapse under me."

"Reckon that's a good idea. My old hoss ain't up to many more miles tonight either."

"We got to push on," Dupree said, his voice rising. "We're exposed out here. The thunderbird kin see us right clearly and swoop on down and—"

"Shut up," Slocum said. "We're camping. If there's water anywhere around here, we camp beside the stream."

"Might be somethin' ahead," Rawlins said. "My hoss is all excited 'bout somethin'."

"The thunderbird," Dupree muttered.

"Ain't nervous. More like expectant." Rawlins looked at Slocum, who nodded, then rode ahead.

Slocum let Rawhide get a dozen yards away before he turned to Dupree and said, "You're spookin' him and getting on my nerves. Not one more word about that bird."

"But—" Dupree clamped his mouth shut when he saw how serious Slocum was.

Slocum knew better than to let fear take hold. Dupree might not be calmed but Slocum wasn't going to let him get Rawlins riled up. They were on the run from the law, and the Sioux were on the warpath. Their painted faces and decorated horses showed that. Those were the two most important dangers they faced—not some imaginary thunderbird.

Slocum saw that Dupree wasn't inclined to argue. He rode off, letting the other cowboy trail him, mumbling as he rode.

"Here it is," Rawlins called. "Knew there had to be some water around, what with my hoss bein' so antsy." Rawhide had dropped to his knees beside the sluggishly flowing stream and took off his hat, filling it with water to douse himself as his horse drank.

Slocum let his gelding drink while he prowled about. He found a fire pit that hadn't been used in months. A careful circuit revealed nothing more to indicate pilgrims had been this way recently.

"Come on over," Slocum called. "We can pitch camp here."

Dupree and Rawlins were skeptical when they saw the old fire pit, then settled down.

"Didn't bring much in the way of tucker," Dupree said. "I was jist glad to git away from the Box M." He chuckled. "Never thought I'd ride away from a good job and rob a bank in the same afternoon."

"That reminds me of the time . . ." Rawhide Rawlins began to spin his yarn.

Slocum slipped from camp and foraged the best he could. This late in the year, there wasn't much in the way food to be had, but he clubbed an incautious rabbit with a rock that gave them a greasy, if small, meal. Keeping the cooking fire low and banked prevented anyone on their trail from spotting the flames, though the odor of cooking meat would draw a posse like flies to shit.

After they had finished, Dupree and Rawlins stretched out and were asleep in seconds. Slocum found it harder to join them. When they got free of this maze of canyons, they had to divvy up the loot and go their separate ways. Neither of the others had a lick of sense when it came to avoiding the law. If they rode together much longer, either Dupree or Rawlins—and Slocum put his bet on Dupree—would do something stupid and land them in the hoosegow.

Getting through the canyons might take days. He vowed to split the money in the morning and tell them to each take a branching canyon. His eyes darted to the burlap bag holding the loot. Rawlins was using it as a pillow. Slocum sat up, resolved to wake them and split the money now. If he headed out right away, no matter how tired his horse was, he could put five miles between them all before sunrise.

He started to call out when he heard strange sounds in the distance, up the canyon where they traveled. His hand flew to his six-shooter when a scream rang out, disturbing the silence.

Both Rawlins and Dupree came instantly awake, Dupree grabbing for his rifle and clutching it to his body.

"What's that? The thunderbird?"

"That was a woman screamin'," Rawlins said. "I oughta know. I've made enough of 'em scream in my day, though usually with pleasure."

"Quiet," Slocum said. He turned slowly and homed in on the woman. The scream had died and was replaced with sobs, as if she tried to contain any sound. "She's in trouble."

"Hell, Slocum, so are we," Rawlins said.

"You two stay here," Slocum ordered.

He started walking, careful of where he stepped. The moon had crossed the sky and now lit the path from behind him. This gave him a decent sense of the trail; it also outlined him to anyone with a six-gun and a thought to use it.

A couple hundred yards saw the path turn sharply and wend through a tumble of rocks close to the canyon wall. The woman's sobs came from that direction. Slocum advanced warily, Colt Navy ready for any trouble. Even as careful as he was, he still fell over the woman.

He came to his knees and turned, his pistol aimed at her in the shadow of a large boulder. All he saw was dark movement. Her sobs had died down, replaced with the scraping of leather against stone.

"Stop moving about like that," Slocum said.

"Don't kill me. Please. I don't want to go back!"

"I'm not going to kill you, and I have no idea what you're talking about."

"You . . . you're not from Wilson's Creek?"

"That a town nearby?"

He saw the darkness fold into itself. She cried openly now.

"I'll do whatever you want. Just get me away from here. Please!"

Slocum scooted about and worked his way closer. From the evidence he could see in the moonlight, she'd been following the rocky trail but had fallen and somehow got her foot wedged under the huge boulder.

"I'm trapped and can't get free," she said.

Slocum slid his six-shooter into the holster. Deciding caution played the best hand, he slid the leather thong over the hammer. If she tried to grab for his gun, it would take a considerable amount of strength or dexterity to get it free.

"You did get yourself stuck good and proper," he said. Her entire foot was hidden in the crevice.

"Oh," she said as he hiked up her skirt and ran his hand down her calf to her ankle. He looked up at her, their faces only inches apart now. She smiled weakly and said, "Do whatever you need to do."

Reaching into his pocket, he pulled out a lucifer and lit it, so he could see the situation a bit better in the temporary light. The woman's face was dirty, smudged from grit and tears, but this couldn't hide how pretty she was. He now saw the bow-shaped red lips, the blush to her cheeks, the long dark hair framing her oval face, which all added to her beauty. Cleaned up, she would turn heads in any town.

"Didn't mean to be forward," Slocum said, blowing out the lucifer and plunging them in semidarkness again. Gently he put his hand back on her bare leg. The flesh trembled. He stroked a bit and calmed her, as he would a nervous filly.

Only when she relaxed and leaned back, supporting

herself on her elbows, did he examine her ankle as best he
could in the dim moonlight. The high-topped shoe had pro-
tected her from serious injury. No bones seemed broken. He
grunted as he slid down farther. His face pressed into her
lap. Again he looked up to see if she objected. If anything,
she had finally found something to enjoy.

"Sorry," he said, not meaning it.

He burrowed down another few inches. He got his fingers
under the arch in her shoe, then straightened his back and
pulled. The foot didn't budge at first. He applied more pressure, keeping it steady rather than jerking. Leather finally
scraped against rock again, but this time her foot moved in
the right direction. She popped free and lay flat on her back.
In a very unladylike move, she brought up her once-trapped
leg and let the skirt fall away, exposing herself all the way
to the thigh.

"I don't think I'm injured. Do you see any cuts?"

Slocum worked back to sit beside her. He watched as she
turned her leg this way and that so he could examine her in
the moonlight.

"You look to be in mighty fine shape, ma'am."

"You're not from Wilson's Creek?"

"Don't know the place."

"I'm Alicia Watson."

"John Slocum," he said, touching the brim of his hat. "If
I might be so bold—"

"Why, you are certainly that, the way you touched my
leg and continue to stare at my uncovered flesh," she said
coyly.

"Who are you running from?"

This dampened her good humor. Tears welled again in
her eyes. She brushed at them and turned her face away.

"If I told you, it would mean nothing but trouble. Please,
help me get away."

"But not back along the trail you just followed?"

"No!" She jerked around. The panic on her lovely face convinced him she was not acting. No one feigned such fear.

"You might consider another road," Slocum said. "Fact is, you might be jumping from the frying pan into the fire if you ride with us."

"Us?"

Slocum whirled about, hand going to his six-shooter. The keeper loop prevented him from drawing. He was glad because he might have thrown down on Rawhide Rawlins and killed the man.

"Why'd you follow me?" Slocum demanded.

"We heard more noises. Spooked Dupree." Rawlins moved closer. "Truth be told, swappin' Lee fer this pretty lady would be quite an improvement. Howdy, ma'am." Rawlins took off his hat and held it in front of him.

"Your partner?" Alicia asked.

He ignored her.

"What noises?" Slocum asked.

"Like before. Or Dupree thought they was like . . . what he thought he saw. Heard."

Slocum got to his feet and started back toward their camp. Alicia let out a tiny bleat. He looked over his shoulder and saw her holding out her hand to be helped to her feet.

"My ankle throbs like an old achy tooth," she said. "I don't want to slow you down none."

"I'll be pleased to help, ma'am," Rawlins said. He pulled her to her feet and caught her as she stumbled.

Slocum wasn't inclined to believe she had twisted the ankle enough to warrant such hobbling, but Rawlins was willing to put his arm around her to help her along.

"You left Dupree alone?"

"Hell, Slocum, ain't nobody else out here, is there?" Rawhide turned and said, "Sorry about the language, ma'am. Tend to get a bit salty when there's nuthin' to do but cuss out your partners and an ole herd of cattle."

Slocum raced along the trail, making better time now that the moonlight shone down on the ground in front of him and he wasn't worried about stumbling across the woman. What did worry him was Dupree and the loot. They had ridden together for six months, and he had no reason to think Dupree would double-cross him and Rawlins, but their world had been turned upside-down all in a single day. It might be enough to convince Dupree he was invincible and deserving of the money from the bank.

The fire had died to embers. Slocum approached with his six-gun ready for action.

"Dupree? Where are you?" No answer. "Lee?"

Slocum cocked his head to one side and heard distant sounds coming from the large canyon branching off to the right of their campsite. He tried to put a name to what he heard. He couldn't. The sounds were muffled and indistinct.

Rawhide and Alicia approached the camp from behind him. He reached down and grabbed the burlap sack filled with greenbacks from the bank. He expected to find it empty. To his surprise, it was plump with stolen money. Dupree hadn't made off with it. He quickly dropped it when Rawlins got closer.

"Where's Dupree?" Rawhide asked.

"Is he your other partner?" Alicia walked without need of a strong shoulder to lean on now.

They all fell silent when a heart-stopping cry of utter fear and pain cut through the night. The stark agony echoed from the canyon walls, then faded away slowly until only silence reigned.

Slocum looked at Rawlins and Alicia. Their faces reflected the horror he felt deep in his gut. They had just heard a man die.

4

"Oh, no," Alicia Watson said in a choked voice. Her hand went to her mouth as she turned away.

"Think that was Dupree doin' all the screamin'?" Rawlins asked.

"Stay here. I'll find out," Slocum said.

He saw no reason to answer Rawlins, not in front of the woman, because he thought his partner was right. No man made a sound like that and lived. And he would bet his share of the money from the robbery that it had been Lee Dupree doing the screaming.

He left camp, dropped to one knee, and scanned the ground for a trail. Why Dupree had left camp at all was a poser, but the tracks showed he had—and had been alone. Slocum considered the possibility that Marshal Hillstrom had snuck up and captured the man, but the death cry was beyond his ken to explain. From all he had heard about the Halliday lawman, he wasn't the kind to drag a prisoner out and then gut him with a hunting knife, just for the hell of it.

Dupree had definitely left camp on his own. Slocum studied either side of the boot prints to see if someone with a rifle might have stood off and forced Dupree to walk along. The ground was devoid of tracks other than from small critters and possibly a bear. Those tracks were old, though.

Dupree might have gone after the bear and tangled with ten-inch-long claws. From the length of his stride, Dupree had hurried along when he left camp. Why the rush? Slocum had to find out. He advanced slowly, keeping the tracks in view until he reached a rocky stretch where he lost the trail.

Kneeling, he looked over the rocks and saw a dark crevice between towering, wind-carved knobby spires that had to be Dupree's destination. Nowhere else afforded a likely trail. Slocum walked slowly to the crevice, turned sideways, and pushed through to find himself at the edge of a large sandy pit. In spite of himself, he caught his breath at the sight of the body.

Dupree had been ripped to bloody shreds.

Slocum tried to find the cause but couldn't. The only tracks in the sand were Dupree's. He edged closer, heart hammering. He tried to catch any sound but even the wind had died down. When he reached Dupree, he rolled the man over. His chest and face were untouched. Deep claw marks on his back showed he had been attacked as he looked away.

He hadn't even tried to run from the look of the tracks. Something had swooped down, raked savagely across his back, and caused the man to cry out in pain and death, then had vanished. Or flown away. Slocum found small traces of claw marks showing where a bird had hopped about in the sandy pit but the size made him wonder if he was mistaken. The claw marks digging into the ground were large enough for a bear.

But there weren't any tracks into the area.

"Something mighty strong and big got you, old partner," Slocum said. He backed away. Burying Dupree would take some effort since he didn't have a shovel. Even if the sand proved as soft down lower as it was on the surface, he couldn't dig fast.

Once he reached the rocky border of the tiny arena, he circled. He found scratches on one rock that would have been behind Dupree as he was attacked. Alongside the grooves dark drops of blood were already dried. Slocum tried to reconstruct the attack. All he could think was a big bird had crouched on this rock, waiting for its prey. A flap of wings, a snap of the beak, and claws flashing. Dupree had died without even seeing his attacker.

Whatever had killed the man had long since left. Slocum settled his pistol in his holster and hunted for a stick to begin digging the grave. He had barely started when gunfire echoed up the canyon.

"Son of a bitch," he cursed, dropping the digging tool and drawing his six-shooter.

More shots followed. He identified at least three different guns. One might have been from Rawlins's rifle, but he couldn't be sure. He ran back along the trail, stumbling in places because the moon had finally dipped behind the mountain peaks. By the time Slocum reached the campsite, the sounds of a gunfight had died down.

The first thing he saw was that their horses were gone. He cursed some more when a quick search failed to turn up the money from the bank robbery. As he rummaged about, he found spent brass from two different rifles. At least Rawlins had put up some fight.

He used his full skills to see that one horse from the camp had gone farther into the canyon where he had found Alicia Watson. A half-dozen riders had come from that direction, then retreated. His best guess was that riders from Wilson's Creek had come after Alicia, had found her, fought with Rawhide, then taken the girl back to town off to the west.

"So what happened to you, Rawhide?"

Slocum saw that another horse had retraced their route, heading eastward. That would take the rider into the arms of the posse—or maybe not. These had to be Rawhide Rawlins's tracks as he rode off to get away from the men who

had taken Alicia. A few shots, a hasty mount, and then Rawlins had ridden away.

With the loot.

A neigh followed by the sound of a hoof scraping across
rock drew Slocum's attention. He homed in, made his way
through the thorny vegetation, and found his horse nervously
awaiting him. Slocum closed the distance slowly, knowing
better than to spook the already anxious horse. He caught
up the bridle and patted the horse's neck before leading it
back to camp.

He swung his saddle over the horse's back, then cinched
the leather straps. The horse was tuckered out from riding
all day, but it had gotten a couple hours of rest. Slocum had
been unable to get any sleep, and now he had to catch up
with Rawlins if he wanted his share of the money.

Leaving Alicia Watson to her fate in Wilson's Creek
bothered him for only a short while. Whatever she ran from,
she could run from again. Lee Dupree had lost that chance.
Rawhide Rawlins was heading back into the posse's guns
and might be in worse shape if the Sioux caught him. As
much as anything, Slocum wanted to ask if Rawlins had
taken the money and ridden away because he thought all his
partners were dead.

Slocum was a good judge of character and doubted Rawhide had double-crossed him. He still wanted his share of
the money. And he wanted to verify his judgment when it
came to Rawlins.

After a quick glance over his shoulder in the direction
Alicia and her captors had taken, Slocum put his heels to
his horse's flanks and headed back toward Halliday.

Slocum awoke with a start when his horse stumbled. He shook
himself and slowly realized he had been asleep in the saddle
for some time. The sun was poking a red edge over the distant
horizon. The mountains behind him took on a red-and-orange
glow as he sat straighter and fought to get his bearings.

Somehow, asleep as he had been, he had managed to follow Rawlins's trail. Plainly visible on the hard ground was a single set of hoofprints going straight for a deserted town not a mile away. Slocum squinted a mite as he scouted for Rawlins. The condition of the buildings told him the town had been deserted a year or more. The harsh winter and hot summer had taken their toll. From the nearness to the hills behind him, this town had likely supplied gold prospectors what they needed to search for the elusive metal. If any mines had been started nearby, they must have petered out and the townspeople had moved on to greener pastures.

Slocum remembered Alicia saying Wilson's Creek was deeper in the rugged territory. The proprietors and barkeeps and whores from this town could have drifted on to Wilson's Creek.

He had no idea what this town was nor did he know diddly-shit about Wilson's Creek. It didn't matter to him since all he wanted was his share of the loot—now half. If Rawhide wanted, they could ride north toward Canada and split later to avoid the posse, but with what he had been through, Slocum wasn't inclined to want a partner riding at his side much of the way.

A shudder passed through him as he remembered how Dupree had been ripped apart. That had been bad, but the lack of tracks around him was downright scary. Involuntarily, Slocum looked up into the clear blue Dakota sky. Not even a buzzard circled above this early.

As he rode closer to the ghost town, he heard a horse protesting. Then he realized the sounds came from at least two horses. That turned him cautious. Rawhide might have fallen into a trap laid by Marshal Hillstrom. For all he knew, it was the only town in this part of the countryside where a man on the run might seek shelter.

When he heard a muffled cry, he cut away from a direct approach and circled, intending to get a better idea of what he was getting himself into. He had ridden in from the west.

Following the contours of the land, partly hiding himself from observation if anyone lay in wait along the main street, he came at the town from the north. Finding a dilapidated livery stable, he put his horse in. Some dried oats remained in an old nosebag, almost falling apart. Slocum knocked this out into a trough and let the horse eat. The gelding would have to go without water until Slocum found out what trouble Rawhide had gotten himself into.

Fitful wind blew through the walls of an abandoned general store, where he slipped in to hide as he took a better look down the main street. The wind carried fine dust with it, making his eyes water. His were the first footprints in the dust on the floor in a long time. That made him more confident that a few townspeople had not stuck around. Anyone else in town, like him and Rawhide, would be passing through and not likely to know the best spots for an ambush.

He peered through the broken windowpane. The wind picked up and carried sound away from him, if he had located the source properly. Twenty yards down the street, a two-story hotel tried to collapse in on itself. The exterior had been built of brick, reflecting the scarcity of lumber out here. What wood had been found ended up shoring mines or being burned to stay warm during the long winters. Leaving his safety in the store, he edged down to the hotel.

The front door creaked open as he shoved against it with his shoulder. He almost tumbled in when it gave way suddenly. Catching himself, he dropped to one knee and swung his six-gun around to cover the hotel's lobby. Another shriek came from a hotel room. Slocum ground his teeth together in frustration.

That was a woman crying out. He might have followed Alicia rather than Rawhide Rawlins and the loot from the robbery. A quick retreat might be smarter than barging in without knowing what he faced. The thought of finding an entire posse scattered throughout the hotel made him wary.

He got to his feet and dashed between the hotel and a

saloon next door. Behind the tumbledown buildings, he found two horses tethered and eyeing each other suspiciously. One was Rawhide's horse. He had never seen the other before.

New cries from inside the hotel drew him back. He passed the strange horse, avoiding a nasty kick from the rear hooves, then went to the hotel's back entrance. Someone had torn the door from its hinges recently. The wood where the metal hinge had been hadn't weathered yet.

"No, stop, don't!"

He edged down the narrow hallway, passing a room all torn up from a recent fight. Slocum moved quicker now. The outer door stood open where he had broken in earlier. At the side of the lobby an overturned settee without one leg showed the hotel owner had no interest in taking all the furniture when he had left. He might have just walked away when the town had died.

"You got real purty intimate parts, girlie."

Slocum spun around in the lobby, then saw narrow stairs going up to what had been the second floor. Three quick steps up brought him to a room lacking an outer wall. The door had been removed, giving him a clear view of everything happening in the room. A cowboy held both of Alicia's wrists in one dirty hand while his other had moved up under her skirts to probe between her thighs. His body pinned her down on the slanting floor.

She fought but he was too strong.

"You don't have to git all wet fer me. I don't care long as you spread them legs wide enough."

"No, no!"

"If you don't, I'll have to rough you up a bit and then do it anyway. I'm kinda hopin' you won't give it up easy like. It's fun whalin' away on whores like you."

Slocum moved into the room. He misjudged the way the floor sloped outward due to the lower story collapsing. He grunted as he fought to keep his balance. The cowboy heard the ruckus, released Alicia, and went for his six-gun. His hand hardly touched the butt when Slocum swung with all his might. The barrel of his Colt Navy collided with the man's temple, sending him staggering. Slocum knew right away it hadn't been a solid hit. He hadn't felt bone break.

The cowboy rolled over to hands and knees and shook his head to clear it.

"You bought yerself a passel o' trouble. I'm a deputy."

The man foolishly tried to drag out his six-shooter. Slocum cocked and fired before the deputy got his hand halfway to his holster. He jerked and fell onto his face. He twitched about like a fish tossed up on a riverbank.

Slocum looked at a horrified Alicia Watson. The woman's blouse had been torn and her skirt was partly ripped off where the man had groped her.

"Look out!"

Slocum fired a second time. This round hit the deputy in the side of the head, just above the spot where Slocum had laid his pistol barrel.

"No question about him being dead this time," Slocum said.

"You killed him," Alicia said in a small voice.

"That shouldn't bother you none," Slocum said, "not after what he was fixing to do."

"*I* wanted to kill him," she said, anger in her voice. "I need the practice if I'm going to kill—"

"Hush!"

Slocum clamped his hand over her mouth and shoved her back so he could see past her out the broken wall. She struggled but he had the advantage of strength and leverage as he pushed her across the cot. She sat heavily. The canvas tore and she ended up with her knees up by her ears and fighting to get free.

"You're as bad as—"

"Shut up! Close your mouth and open your ears."

"I—" Alicia glared at him as she flopped onto her side and pulled herself free of the rotted cot.

When she got to her feet, standing in the corner of the room, she started to berate him again. Then her eyes went wide. She mouthed, "More?"

Slocum nodded. He didn't know how many were riding into town, but from the sound carried on the wind, there were more than he could fight. He motioned for her to follow him back into the corridor. She stooped, grabbed the deputy's six-shooter from its holster, then took the time to rip off a badge from his coat lapel. With a backhand throw, she tossed it outside. Only then did she press close to Slocum and ask, "What do we do?"

"You know how to use that?" He tapped the six-gun with his. The metallic click rang loud in his ears.

"If anyone gets close enough so I can jam the muzzle into their guts, I can't miss."

Slocum knew marksmanship was the least of using a six-gun. Killing a man required an inclination most peaceful folks didn't appreciate. From the set of her jaw and the coldness in her brown eyes, he decided taking the gun from her would be difficult, if not deadly for him—and that answered his objections to her keeping the stolen pistol.

He stepped out onto the back stairs, only to have them yield under him. Slocum thrust out his arm as much to keep his balance as to force Alicia back into the hotel out of sight. Two lawmen looked over Rawlins's and the dead deputy's horses. And riding up were three more. A ray of sunshine caught the badge on the lead rider's chest. They were caught inside the hotel as the posse assembled out back.

5

"We can shoot our way out!" Alicia cried.

Slocum kept pushing her back along the askew corridor until they were out of earshot of the deputies. When the marshal joined them in examining the horses, a half dozen of the posse would be able to train their guns on the hotel. With the brick walls in sad shape and the wood doors mostly rotted, there wasn't any way he and Alicia could fight.

"We don't shoot it out with the law, not after I just killed a deputy."

"He said he was hunting for bank robbers from over in Halliday."

Slocum didn't answer. If killing a deputy intent on raping her wasn't a good enough excuse for avoiding the rest of the posse, nothing would satisfy her. With Alicia's bloodthirsty promise to kill anyone getting in her way, he wasn't sure the law wouldn't be as interested in taking her prisoner as it was in getting the bank money back.

"I can explain he was trying to hurt me," she said.

Slocum stared at her. The deputy wanted to do more than

hurt her. After he'd raped her, he would have killed her and left her body for the coyotes.

"You go ahead and try that," he said. "Tell them you killed the deputy."

"But it would have been in self-defense. And you were only protecting me."

Slocum returned to the stairs leading to the lobby. The staircase had collapsed. He looked around for some way out. Only blue sky showed where the roof should have been. Keeping the high ground might have made sense if he'd had the firepower to hold off the posse. And if Dupree and Rawlins had been with him, they might all have had a chance of potshotting the lawmen.

"Hang on," he said. He grabbed Alicia around the waist and stepped out where the stairs had been. They crashed to the lower floor. She struggled but he kept her from running off in panic.

"Help me," he whispered in her ear. "If you don't, we're both dead."

He kicked away a pile of bricks and found what he sought. A few floorboards had been broken down into a cellar. Yanking away another board, he wedged himself in, then twisted and fell about five feet. He bent low and got under the lobby flooring. Looking up at Alicia, he thought she might have been an angel.

Sunlight caught her mussed brunette hair and turned it into a chocolate halo around her dirty face. Her torn blouse revealed just a touch of bare breast, but her ripped skirts showed her legs all the way to her thighs. It hadn't been that long ago that Slocum had run his hands along those calves, found the foot jammed under the rock, and freed her back in the hills. In spite of his predicament, he found himself wondering what it would be like to run his hands along those legs again, up the thighs and—

"Move over. They're coming!"

She kicked at him with the foot he had been fantasizing

about, and he got out of the way so she could drop into the cellar alongside him. She scuttled away as he worked the plank he had pushed free back into place. Seconds after he got it lined up with the other floorboards, footsteps approached with drumlike precision on the planks. Jingling spurs and a few grunts warned him the posse had arrived—directly over his head.

He started to move back but the board refused to stay in place. As boot steps came closer, their gait uneven, he pushed upward with all his strength until he supported a man's weight. Whoever had come into the lobby stood on the loose plank, not knowing Slocum was all that kept him from tumbling into the cellar.

"They got to be somewhere," came the deep voice.

"Marshal Hillstrom, lookee in here. Tunley's dead. Shot dead!"

Slocum gasped in relief as the weight disappeared off the plank. He would have sagged down and let the floorboard fall if Alicia hadn't reached across, pressing into his back to hold the board. He didn't mind the feel of her so close, but their situation was dire.

"How long before they find us?" she whispered.

"They'll have blood in their eye now that they've found the dead deputy."

Alicia craned her neck and looked up to the lobby.

"They're all in the room. We can escape."

Slocum had another idea. He propped up the board to keep the marshal from seeing right away where his quarry had hidden. Sitting and looking around the dusty cellar, he pointed toward the rear of the building. Alicia obeyed immediately, crawling over the debris to a break in the foundation near the back door. Slocum pushed her out of the way and looked up. A slow smile came to him. Luck was finally with them.

Pulling down the brick and concrete opened a crawl space large enough for him to squeeze through. Alicia reached up for him to help her out of the cellar, but he ignored her. He moved among the horses, gathering reins.

"You could have given me a hand up," she said, climbing out of the cellar and brushing off her skirt. All she did was smear the dirt more.

"Mount up," Slocum said. "Take the reins of the horses and don't let even one of them go free."

Alicia wiped grit from her eyes, blinked, and then said, "We'll be horse thieves."

Arguing the merit of horse thievery against being hanged for killing a deputy could wait. Slocum vaulted onto the nearest horse, brought it under control, and immediately rode for the stable where he had left his gelding. Alicia muttered but came after him. Barely had Slocum reached the livery and pulled his horse out when lead began flying.

"Ride!"

Slocum put his head down and snapped the reins to bring his horse to a gallop. He slowed when he heard Alicia cry out. He looked back to see her sitting on the ground. She had been pulled off her horse by the horses she led. The posse's mounts had scattered, spooked by the gunfire, and ran in all directions.

He slowed, turned, and snared the reins of Rawlins's horse, which Alicia had ridden, and went back for her. The marshal and his men ran from the town, shooting as they came. If they had stopped to take aim, Slocum might have been filled with lead. Instead, their shots all went wild.

"Come on," Slocum said, reaching down. He caught her wrist and yanked her into the air. She landed hard behind him. "Get on your horse." He pulled Rawlins's mount up against his knee.

Alicia moved with a greater show of horsemanship than he'd expected. She settled in the saddle.

"It won't take them long to round up their horses," he said.

"Holding on to a half-dozen reins was more difficult than I thought."

Blaming her accomplished nothing. They had to get away. Reluctantly Slocum turned back toward the mountains.

"No, we need help. You can't go back there!" Alicia cried.

When she tried to veer away, Slocum headed her off and herded her into the maze of canyons they had left.

"You're crazy. They—"

"The marshal is behind us."

"I need to tell him about—"

Slocum made certain she didn't ride back by snatching the reins from her and leading her horse. He had followed her thinking she was Rawhide Rawlins. He had to find out what happened in the canyon, to his partner and to the loot from the bank. Alicia had to know something since she'd been in camp with Rawhide when the gunfire had broken out, drawing Slocum away from burying Dupree.

Alicia rode in stony silence until they reached the juncture of the three canyons. Ahead lay the abandoned camp. To the right, Dupree's body likely had been picked clean by coyotes, buzzards, and insects. And the canyon stretching before him had to be where Rawhide and the loot were to be found.

"We . . . we shouldn't stay here. They'll find us," Alicia said with a quaver in her voice.

"What happened here after Dupree screamed? I heard gunfire and came back to find the camp empty."

Slocum's eyes moved to the spot where Dupree had laid his head on the bag of money. It came as no surprise that the money was still missing.

"He's dead, isn't he? Dupree? It was the thunderbird that got him."

"He's dead," Slocum said, but he didn't want to argue with the woman about the existence of mythological birds any more than he had with Dupree. If anything, Dupree had a stronger argument to make, but Slocum still thought he had tangled with a bear.

Even if he couldn't figure how a bear had entered that sandy pit and left without leaving distinct tracks.

"Rawhide said he heard riders coming. From the direction of Wilson's Creek. I couldn't let them catch me again."

"Why are you running from that town?"

"It's run by a man name of Mackenzie. He's plumb loco but he rules that town with an iron grip."

Alicia's eyes went wide with fear when a loud screech echoed down the canyon in front of them—the one leading to Wilson's Creek, where Slocum thought Rawhide had gone.

"Ignore it," Slocum said. "Why'd Rawhide ride off the way he did?"

"They were Mackenzie's men coming after me. I saddled up and jumped on the nearest horse. Rawhide said he'd keep them from ever catching me. I . . . I rode off just as they circled him. They got the drop on him, but he started shooting. That's all I know."

"You didn't see him gunned down?"

"I was riding away too fast for that. He might have got away, but there were at least three of Mackenzie's gunmen." Alicia flinched when the screech echoed down the canyon again, the hideous sound bouncing from one canyon wall to another. She wrapped her arms around herself and shook as if she'd come down with the ague. "That's the thunderbird. He claims he's got it all caged and lets it loose to kill his enemies."

"Mackenzie? But you said he's loco."

"Dupree was all ripped up, wasn't he? I can tell by the way you talk about him. Nobody human did that. It's Mackenzie's thunderbird."

In spite of himself Slocum asked, "Where'd he get this thunderbird?"

"Don't know. Might be from all the Sioux he's killed.

Mackenzie hates Indians. Heard one of his men say it was because the Sioux killed his entire family."

"That what drove him crazy?"

Alicia shook her head. "No, it's something else. But he's not loco enough to just let the thunderbird go free. He controls it. He turns it against the Indians if they get too close to town."

"You ever see this thunderbird?" Slocum began to get irritated as the screeching grew louder. That might frighten off the Indians or even Alicia Watson, but it only made him more inclined to find who made the noise and silence them for good.

"I've seen what it does. I can't imagine how horrible it must be. Some say that if you stare at the thunderbird, you're a goner. It's born in a thundercloud and rides on storm winds and can even shoot lightning bolts out of its eyes."

"Otherwise, it just claws up men like a bear. There are bears in the Badlands, aren't there?"

"Of course there are," Alicia said, her lips thinning to a razor slash. "But why don't you believe me when I tell you there's a thunderbird?"

Slocum had never put much stock in the supernatural. He had found most things died if you put a bullet through their heart.

"Let's see," he said, tapping his heels on his horse's flanks.

"No, you can't. You'll be killed!"

He looked at her drawn expression. Real fear made her recoil and lean so that she almost fell from her horse.

"What were you running from in Wilson's Creek? What did Mackenzie try to do to you?"

"You can guess. I refuse to—never mind. I'm not going back there. And," she said, a catch in her voice, "I don't want to see you killed either."

This surprised him.

"Why not?"

"You saved me back in that ghost town when you didn't have to. I don't care if you thought you were coming after your partner. You risked your neck to save mine."

"That's not what was at risk," he said. This got a weak smile from her. "It's not going to hurt to rest here, water the horses, then decide what to do."

She dismounted and led the horse toward the small stream. He watched as she went. That was one good-looking woman. He stepped down and let his gelding drink next to the one that had belonged to Dupree. Finding out as much as he could about Wilson's Creek meant the difference between life and death for him. Maybe Rawlins was still alive. If so, Slocum needed to know as much as possible about what his partner might have gotten mixed up in.

That was only a faint hope of finding Rawhide alive, and he knew it. More likely, riding to Wilson's Creek, he would come across Rawlins's body. That meant Mackenzie's henchmen had the money from the bank robbery. Getting it back would take as much information as Alicia could tell him.

Before he could ask her about the town, a new caterwaul made her wince. Alicia turned away and ignored him when he asked about Mackenzie.

He shrugged it off, then stood and walked a few paces off to see what moved around deeper in the canyon. The inhuman cries died down. Slocum waited to see if riders came rushing down on the heels of the shrieks.

"How far is the town?" Slocum asked.

He half turned and then sharp pain lanced through his head. He staggered back. Then came another blow that drove him flat onto his back, unconscious. When he woke up, he thought dynamite had been planted between his ears, then detonated. Forcing his eyes to focus, he looked around.

A new howl from the canyon mouth was his only companion. Alicia and Rawlins's horse were gone.

6

Slocum dunked his head in the stream and came up, shaking like a wet dog. The pain eased and let him think more clearly. Riding toward the bird caws deeper in the canyon might not be the smartest move he ever considered, but Rawlins had gone that way with the bank money. All he wanted was to get his share, then leave the Dakotas as fast as his horse could take him.

He studied the ground and saw that Alicia had ridden into the canyon where Dupree had been killed. He considered her motives, then decided she was telling him the truth—or the truth as she saw it. The screeches in the one canyon had forced her to choose a different route. Retracing her tracks to the ghost town would take her into the arms of the law. She might be a good enough liar to deny knowing anything about the dead deputy, but Slocum had seen the fire in her eyes when she spoke of the man who had tried to rape her in the old hotel. Alicia would give herself away and likely in ways she never thought of.

If the marshal saw her with the pistol, he'd probably recognize it as the dead deputy's. Alicia's wrists would be clamped into irons and she'd languish in the Halliday jail.

Knowing it was foolish, but lying enough to himself that he needed what she knew of Wilson's Creek to find Rawlins, he mounted and rode after her. From the sun in the sky, he had been knocked out for close to a half hour, giving her a big head start. Rather than pushing his horse to overtake her, he rode steadily, keeping a sharp lookout for the bear that had killed Dupree—and Mackenzie's henchmen. That part of Alicia's story rang true.

Slocum had seen enough towns run by a fast gun. Fear controlled most of the population, and a small army of gunmen always shot first and thought later. That kept the ordinary citizens cowed. In this part of the Badlands, Wilson's Creek must have developed as a mining town. It might have been where the populace from the one to the east had moved when new gold strikes had been made. Men always sought the quick riches, the easy wealth.

He passed the sandy pit where Dupree's body had been, drew rein, and halted to study the matter a bit more. His earlier suspicion had proven true. Dupree's corpse had been well gnawed, and ants worked on it now that the larger carrion eaters had eaten their fill. Slocum hunted for any bear scat, and slowly a question came to him that he hadn't considered before.

If a bear had killed Dupree, why hadn't it bothered to eat him? The lack of tracks other than a few deep claw marks in the sand was curious, but the bear had not had much of a fight, not attacking Dupree from the back. Slocum remembered that Dupree's six-shooter had been in his holster, so he hadn't angered the bear with a stray shot.

Slocum had seen bullets bounce off a bear's skull. That could make any creature furious if it didn't kill it outright. But the bear had struck from behind.

Had it even been a bear? There was no way a black bear or grizzly killed a man without leaving more trace in the sand. In spite of himself, Slocum mentally pictured a huge bird swooping down as Dupree looked away. Talons flashing, the thunderbird would have killed before the man even knew he was dead.

Slocum snorted. There wasn't any such thing. What was real existed all around him, where he could see it, feel it, and shoot it.

He snapped about, eyes going to the canyon wall on his right. Being lost in his speculation about a thunderbird had turned him careless. A bit of luck allowed him to see Alicia's tracks cutting to a narrow trail that led up to the rim. She was trying to escape the maze of canyons.

Turning his horse to the narrow trail, he studied the signs for a full minute to make out a muddled set of hoofprints. Alicia's horse went up, but another set of boot prints was almost as recent. He rode a few yards up the path to the point where the boot prints stopped suddenly. It was as if the man had walked this far and evaporated. While it seemed incredible, whoever had left that set of tracks had jumped from the trail to the top of a huge boulder.

Slocum let out a low whistle of disbelief. To reach the rock, the man had to jump a full twenty feet. Slocum had seen men in his day capable of incredible feats, but nothing like this. And from the likeliest rock to the sandy pit where Dupree had died was another thirty feet. All Slocum had seen on the ground, rocky though it was, had been Alicia's tracks.

He dismounted and looked more closely at the boot prints. The toes had dug in deeper than the heels, showing the man had jumped. Slocum looked up slowly and doubted anyone could make it to the nearest rock. He studied the ground almost thirty feet below. The man ought to have landed and broken every bone in his body. The vegetation showed no trace of being disturbed by a body crashing down from a great height.

A horse neighing farther along the steeply curving trail made Slocum lean out precariously to see the switchback fifty feet above his head. He heard soft sounds, possibly Alicia cursing, then a stone tumbled down past him. Someone was ahead of him on the upper part of the trail, and it was probably the woman.

He walked his horse around the sharp turn and saw the back half of a horse on the trail a hundred feet ahead. Trudging up the slope, he halted to get a better idea of what he faced. The horse stood half in a cave. Alicia didn't appear to be on the trail, so she had to be in the cave. Slocum secured his horse's reins to a rock and edged forward, not wanting to spook the other horse. It remembered him and only pawed a bit at the hard rock cave floor.

Alicia sat inside, holding her head in her hands and sobbing quietly.

He slipped past the horse and watched her. It took the woman a few seconds to realize she had company. When her head came up, her eyes flashed open and a tiny gasp escaped her lips.

"You shouldn't have left me like that," Slocum said. "There's more going on in these canyons than meets the eye." His thoughts flashed to Dupree dying in such a bloody fashion and the untouched ground around his corpse. He pushed back his Stetson to show the lump where she had clobbered him. "Hurts like hell."

"I can't go back to Wilson's Creek. I was a slave there and so were—" She bit off the rest of her words.

"You being used there? By this Mackenzie?"

She shook her head and slowly said, "I was lucky. He hadn't got around to me, but he would have."

"Your family wasn't so lucky, were they?"

She jumped as if he had stuck her.

"It's not hard figuring out why you're so upset. You got away, they didn't. You want to get somebody to save them."

"That's why I need to fetch the cavalry and wipe out every last one of those outlaws."

"And Mackenzie? You want the Army to take him

prisoner?" He watched her reaction. He doubted she was a good enough actress to pretend the stark hatred he saw in her eyes. He knew the emotions filling her. "You want to kill him yourself."

"I'll shoot him or cut his throat or strangle him. It doesn't matter. I want him dead, and I want to do it for what he's done."

"Explaining that might have gone a ways toward me letting you go," Slocum said.

Her bow-shaped lip curled into a sneer. She shook her head hard enough to dislodge the grimy brunette strands. Without consciously thinking, she pushed the hair back out of her eyes. The hatred burned even brighter now as she thought on Mackenzie.

"Don't lie to me," she said. "You want to find your partner, the one that rode off to Wilson's Creek after maybe throwing in with Mackenzie's men, and you want me to help you. I won't."

Slocum wondered if Rawlins would ride along willingly—or if Mackenzie's men would allow it. That Alicia had broached the idea meant that more about Wilson's Creek had to be unearthed before he rode in and got himself killed.

"Might be we can join forces. I can find my partner and help you get your family out." He saw the change in her attitude. A touch of doubt replaced the hatred there before. Slocum bent over, put his finger under her chin, and lifted her face upward.

He kissed her. For a moment, she resisted, then the kiss became mutual. Alicia threw her arms around his neck and pulled him down to sit beside her. They shifted about, and during the preliminary mating dance, Slocum shucked off his cross-draw holster, tossed aside his hat, and added Alicia's blouse to the pile.

"Don't stop," she said as he ran his finger along her jaw, across her throat with its throbbing vein, and then lower to the deep valley between her breasts.

She shrugged her shoulders and pulled her torn chemise down, leaving her naked to the waist. For a moment he only stared at the white mounds of succulent flesh. There was a great deal to appreciate. The twin mounds of tit were firm and white, delicately veined with blue. Capping each grew a pink nipple, hardening with her arousal. He pulled her closer, but Alicia reached up and laced her fingers behind his head, moving his face down into the deep, warm canyon.

He got the idea. His tongue flicked out to tease and torment, then he moved from the valley between to the summit on her left breast. Sucking hard, he drew the nip between his lips and then pressed his tongue down hard, mashing it into the softness of the breast beneath. Alicia gasped and thrust her chest forward in an effort to stuff more into his mouth.

Slocum used his teeth to rake along the tender sides. Then his tongue soothed. He finally blew gently. The evaporation sent shivers throughout her body. Her body had been tense. Now it melted.

Slocum followed her backward, his mouth never letting up on the oral assault he gave to every part of her chest. One tit to the other, playing with her nipples, sucking, biting, licking, he did everything until she sobbed with the stark pleasure of it all.

"More," she said. "Your mouth is wonderful, John, but I want more."

He ran his hands under her skirts and pushed upward, stroking along the insides of her thighs. Every touch sent a new tremor through her body. As he pushed the unwanted cloth out of the way to expose her most intimate regions, she rocked back and lifted her knees on either side of his body.

But he had other ideas. Rather than slide forward and enter her, he got his shoulder under her knees and lifted her legs high, causing her to wantonly expose herself.

"You liked my mouth before? How about now?" He

thrust his face at the juncture of her thighs and licked the pinkly scalloped sex lips from bottom to top.

A shriek of pure delight rewarded his efforts. His tongue flashed about, then worked its way between her nether lips into her heated core. He pressed a thumb down on the tiny pink spire rising at the top of her sex lips and diddled it as he strove to shove his tongue as far into her heated core as possible. For a moment, he became blind and deaf. Her strong thighs clamped on either side of his head, holding him in place.

His efforts never flagged. He moved his left arm around to the small of her back and lifted her hips so he could gain easier access. Tongue flicking about like a snake's, he soon caused her to arch her back even more and cry out in release. The death-lock of her legs around his head eased.

As she relaxed, he moved to get up on his knees. He kept his shoulders firmly under her legs as he popped the fly buttons on his jeans and let his manhood rush out.

Her eyes flickered open as she said, "That was so good. I—aieee!"

She cried out as he leaned forward, bending her double as he shoved forward. His shaft entered the exact spot where his tongue had been only seconds earlier. It was his turn to gasp as he sank balls deep and felt her tight and hot and damp all around him. For a few seconds, he relished the feel about him, then he pulled back slowly. Inch by inch he withdrew until only the bulbous head of his manhood remained within her.

Easing up on the pressure he applied to her legs, he looked down at her lovely face. A tiny smile crept to the corners of her mouth. Her eyes opened and stared directly at him, challenging him, demanding more.

He gave it to her. He bent her back again and drove even deeper into her gripping center. He began stroking slowly, evenly, entering and retreating at the same pace. She tensed when he was entirely hidden within, squeezing down sensuously on him. This easy motion kept up until friction mounted along his length, goading him to thrust faster. Slocum was dripping in sweat by the time he pistoned fiercely and then lost control.

She cried out again and clutched at his forearms, her fingernails cutting into his flesh. Neither noticed the tiny wounds as release totally possessed them both.

Slocum rocked back and surrendered her legs. They lowered to either side of his body, and she reached down to stroke along his shaft as it melted within her and finally slipped free. No amount of coaxing could get him ready again, not this fast. He wished it could be different.

Never had he seen a woman so lovely. Her cheeks were flushed with a glow that extended all the way down to the tops of her breasts. Her parted lips beckoned, but he couldn't deliver. Not yet. Soon, but not right now.

He rolled across her and lay on the rocky ground next to her. She took his hand and placed it on a bare breast.

"I've never come like that before," she said in a small voice. "You surprised me."

"Riding night herd gave me a lot of time to think about what to do with a pretty woman," he said.

"You must have been on the range a *very* long time," she teased. "Or you have a *very* active imagination."

"There wasn't any imagining what we just done." He squeezed down on her breast, her hand atop his.

"We can be very good together," she said.

Slocum had been in the saddle too long without sleep. This lovemaking had taken the rest of the starch out of him. He wanted to stare at her and drink in her loveliness, but his eyelids sagged and eventually betrayed him.

When he awoke, she was gone again. This time she hadn't slugged him with a rock. All things considered, he preferred this way for her to sneak away from him.

7

Slocum stretched, settled his gun belt, then studied the dirt on the narrow path leading to the canyon rim. Alicia had pressed on to reach the summit. He considered following her again. The dalliance in the shallow cave had not been expected, but it had been worth Slocum's time and then some. In spite of their going in separate directions, he and Alicia had come together in a most satisfying way. Trying to guess what she had gone through in Wilson's Creek proved a fool's game, but Slocum had some idea how men like Mackenzie ran their towns.

It was never pretty for anyone not on the fastest gun's side. She had dropped hints enough to make Slocum wary of the man. The word "loco" was tossed around a lot but too often fit exactly. Alicia intended to fetch soldiers and get them to raid Wilson's Creek. Slocum had to avoid Mackenzie, find Rawhide and the loot, then hightail it out of there.

Slocum smiled ruefully. All he had to do was avoid a crazy gunman, rescue his partner, find the money from the bank, and then get the hell out before the cavalry rode down on the town. He didn't know if Marshal Hillstrom had put out the word of the bank robbery, but Slocum couldn't risk it. Wilson's Creek had to be a quick visit.

He smiled a bit more as he told himself that rescuing Alicia's family wouldn't be a bad thing either. If he got the chance.

Walking slowly back down the steep trail leading his horse, he reached the canyon floor, mounted, and rode steadily for the canyon junction. Fog had settled in, making it impossible to see more than a few yards. This cloaked him, but it also made it more likely he would ride up on Mackenzie's sentries and get caught. Waiting for the fog to lift worried him a mite.

He had no idea where the cavalry post might be or if the post commander might jump to rescuing Alicia's family right away. She had a way about her that a lonely officer out on the frontier might want to favor. She might be a day or two reaching the fort, then another few days returning. Slocum reckoned he had forty-eight hours to get Rawhide to spill his guts about what had happened and where the money they'd stolen was and then have a safe margin to get the hell out of town before the cavalry showed up.

Letting his horse pick its way through the fog took him into a strange world robbed of sound. The mist dampened everything but the clicking of the gelding's horseshoes on the rocky trail. Slocum wiped at his face occasionally as if he sweat. The seasons were changing, and it ought to be cooler in the canyon, but the rock walls held in the day's heat and the fog made it sultry.

A moving phantasm a few feet to his right caused Slocum to go for his six-shooter. He watched as the rider stayed on a steady course, face forward, never giving a hint he had spotted anyone else in the fog. The sound of the passing horse was smothered quickly, once more leaving Slocum isolated in the gray mist. He let his six-shooter drop back into his holster and continued riding. If the other man had left Wilson's Creek, that meant the town was somewhere ahead, and likely not too far off.

Another half-hour's ride brought him to a stretch of canyon with only patches of fog. The sun dropped fast in front of him, almost hidden behind tall peaks. He pressed his horse to the left to hug the canyon wall. If sentries had been posted on the canyon rim, he would be more difficult to see at the base.

The canyon widened and blossomed into a small meadow with what he took to be Wilson's Creek smack in the middle. Not a mile on the other side of the town the hills were dotted with tailings from mines. Faint pick and hammer clicks and clanks reached him, even at this distance, giving some credence to part of Alicia's story. He hadn't really doubted anything she'd said about the town or the mines, but it made him more comfortable to scout it for himself.

One odd thing struck him as he surveyed the road leading from the canyon into town. Twin wooden watch towers had been built. He squinted as he made out two men in each tower. At this time of day, riding into the sun, he would be spotted more easily. Worse, they had battlements to crouch behind in case a skirmish broke out. That would be a potent deterrent to a cavalry charge should Alicia return with the troopers the way he had just ridden.

More defenses than the two towers along the road were scattered around Wilson's Creek. Other points had been fortified in rocks at the canyon mouth. A dozen men could hold off a small army if they had ammunition enough. If the cavalry attacked, they had to filter through the canyon two or three abreast at the most, making them easy targets. Alicia had to warn any officer of the problem and have the soldiers infiltrate before the main attack.

Slocum had to assume the cavalry would attack, even though he suspected even Alicia's charms might not be enough to have an entire company sent out to arrest Mackenzie. The woman had to present overwhelming proof that outlaws were hiding here or that Mackenzie committed crimes and thumbed his nose at the law. Considering the crimes most likely to occur, Marshal Hillstrom might be more interested.

With only a half-dozen men in the posse, he stood no chance at all of breaching the town's defenses. He and his deputies would be more unfortunates who were simply swallowed by the Dakota Badlands.

While he watched, trying to figure out a way of sneaking in, Slocum saw something peculiar. As the sun dipped low and twilight seized the town, the sentries in the towers abandoned their posts. He had already seen two men in each tower; there had actually been four. The eight men trooped along the road back to town, leaving the road undefended.

Slocum strained to see if sentries elsewhere along the canyon walls became more alert. To his surprise, those in the rocks and a few up on the rim made their way to town also, leaving the town undefended. By the time darkness was complete and only bright stars provided illumination to the land, every last guard had vanished into Wilson's Creek.

He waited for the night guards to come out. After an hour when no one did, Slocum mounted and rode slowly into town, keeping well away from the road. The going was rocky until a few hundred yards from the edge of the town, where grassy patches became more common. Rather than riding down the town's main street, Slocum dismounted again and advanced on foot, cautiously peering around the corners of buildings.

Wilson's Creek consisted of ramshackle half-permanent wooden buildings and tents. At the far end of the street, a two-story hotel dominated the town. From within the hotel came raucous laughter. Occasionally armed men emerged and looked around as if hunting for someone, then went back inside. This puzzled Slocum since the saloon in a tent across from his vantage point didn't seem to be the center of their attention.

Men didn't patrol the streets. Everyone remained inside the buildings and tents. After three gunmen came out of the hotel, made their cursory inspection, and went back inside,

Slocum acted. He walked steadily across the street, not hurrying but not creeping either. The last thing he wanted was to draw attention to himself by unusual behavior.

He pushed aside the tent flap and got a blast of cigar smoke in response. A piano at the back of the saloon had seen better days. The piano player sat with a pretty serving girl on his lap, more interested in what she whispered laughingly in his ear than in banging away at the keys. That suited Slocum just fine.

He went straight to the bar, a long wooden plank dropped across a pair of sawhorses. Whiskey bottles were stacked on the ground behind the barkeep, a man with a walrus mustache and a booming laugh. He worked from one end of the bar and back, pouring shots, now and then drawing a weak-looking beer without foam, and always quick with a reply to his customers' jibes.

Slocum didn't push his way through the crowd along the bar. He touched his pockets and realized he had damned little money. It had been the end of the season, and because he'd assumed the Box M owner would pay him not only his salary but a bonus, he hadn't conserved his money when it came to spending. The last poker game in the bunkhouse had about cleaned him out.

But it had been all right since Holman was going to pay for a successful drive.

That thought angered him anew. He looked around for Rawhide Rawlins but didn't see the man. Rawhide had the money to buy his way into an outlaw hideout. He hadn't seen another saloon, so that meant Rawhide likely was in a whorehouse or at the hotel down the street—likely both a hotel and whorehouse with a bar.

The jovial barkeep came over and stared straight at him. Slocum worried that the man knew the regulars and would raise an alarm over a stranger. That didn't happen.

"What's yer poison, sir?"

The politeness startled Slocum. He couldn't afford even a nickel beer but to say so would draw attention.

"I understand you have a way of getting liquor in exchange for—" He'd intended to say "work," thinking he could trade a shift or two as a bouncer for whiskey. The man nearest him interrupted and kept him from being the butt of jokes—or worse.

Such an armed camp had to be under Mackenzie's tight control. Anything that drew attention also drew danger.

"He's challengin' you fer that free bottle of hooch, Axel! Hey, boys, we got a challenge!"

Everyone in the tent fell silent, then the piano player dumped the pretty saloon girl off his lap and began banging out "Camptown Races." The crowd sang along at the top of their lungs as they crowded around Slocum and pushed him forward to bang against the bar. Glasses and mugs rattled the entire length of the plank.

"Challenge, challenge!" the men chanted as the piano player finished his song and came over to get a better view.

"You got the look of a man who can win," the piano player said.

"What do I have to do?" Seeing the man's face flash confusion, Slocum hastily added, "Exactly. I don't want to violate any of the rules."

"Simple enough. You put a slug through Axel's nickel, you win a bottle of whiskey."

The barkeep took a coin out of his vest pocket and held it between thumb and forefinger. Without hesitation, Slocum drew, cocked his Colt, and fired.

The crowd gasped. Axel grabbed his hand and rubbed the fingers used to hold the nickel.

"You damn fool. I was jist showin' the crowd the coin. You was supposed to shoot it after I stuck it to the wall." The barkeep pointed to a spot behind him where a half-dozen holes in the canvas let in fresh air from outside.

"You only git one shot," the piano player said. "Too bad. You got to pay up. A hunnerd dollars."

"That's a mighty lopsided bet," Slocum said, the six-gun still in his hand.

"Mr. Mackenzie says otherwise. You better pay up or you'll be tossed out of Wilson's Creek right now."

A shudder passed through the camp. Men began whispering. The fear this simple punishment caused among hard-bitten men made Slocum wonder what the hell was going on.

"Hey, Axel, this here's the nickel. I found it in the dirt." A burly man at the far end of the bar held up a shiny coin. "Drilled it fair and square. You're the one what gots to pay up."

The coin made its way down the bar, passing from hand to hand until it fell to the plank in front of Slocum.

"He ain't no winner. The bet's to cut the middle out of the nickel. His slug tore off part of the rim. Got to see the hole surrounded by nuthin' but metal."

The piano player picked up the coin and ran his thumb over the rough spot where the bullet had torn the rim and left a small gap.

"You're damned lucky he didn't miss and blow off yer fingers, Axel. I say he won the bet. Don't you all agree? All of you?" He held up the coin with the hole through it so everyone in the saloon could see. The cheer that went up gave Slocum a touch of hope he might get out of this without shooting any of the customers.

The barkeep brushed dirt off his mustache, grumbled a mite, then put a bottle of whiskey down on the bar with a loud clank. Slocum held his breath. There was deathly quiet in the tent, and he knew why.

"What's that?" he demanded of the barkeep.

"What you won, dammit."

"I want shot glasses for everyone here," Slocum said. The deafening cheer told him he had said the right thing. Everyone crowded close to get a shot of free whiskey.

Slocum hung back. The tarantula juice would go a ways toward cutting the taste of trail dust, but it was more important to keep the men from gossiping about him. Let them say they had drunk a free shot, and nobody else in town was likely to ask more than that. If he had denied them their bounty, word might have spread like lightning.

He finally got a shot from the dregs. The liquor burned like a branding iron all the way down to his empty gut, where it threatened to sear away at his flesh the rest of the night.

"You're mighty good with that hogleg, mister," the piano player said. "Ain't seen you around. Mr. Mackenzie jist bring you in?"

"Just got into town," Slocum said.

He didn't understand why the piano player reached out and pushed up Slocum's hat until his forehead was exposed any more than he did what the piano player said next.

"Sorry, sir. Didn't mean nuthin' by my impudence." The man backed off and even put a protective arm around the woman who had been occupying his lap earlier.

They cast quick, fearful looks at Slocum and returned to the piano. In a thrice, the music started again, the man playing and the woman warbling off-key. But no one in the saloon thought twice about it. They had their free drinks.

Slocum had some questions he wanted to ask, but there wasn't anyone to answer. He settled down in a chair and quickly had the table all to himself. The patrons avoided him just as the piano player had, sometimes casting a quick look in his direction, as if to be sure he wasn't swinging his six-gun into action against them.

This set Slocum to thinking. None of the men in the saloon wore sidearms. More than a few carried knives sheathed in boots or at their side, but he was the only one wearing a gun. That struck him as unusual but not to the point of them shunning him.

He looked up when a new customer came into the tent, standing for a moment holding the flap and them moving in quickly. Slocum sat a little straighter in his chair when he saw the man had a number 10 whitewashed on his forehead.

He wore a six-gun slung low, tied down, and moved with the easy grace of a natural shootist.

The others in the tent subtly edged away from him, too. He got a drink, turned, and saw Slocum. A look of relief passed quickly, replaced with a touch of fear that made no sense in a man who likely made his living killing others with the pistol at his side. He came over.

"Mind if I set myself down, sir?"

Slocum indicated he could.

"I swear, them varmints treat me like I was the Grim Reaper himself." The words had hardly escaped when he looked up, eyes going wide with more than a touch of fear. "Didn't mean nuthin' by that, sir."

"Ten?" Slocum asked, tapping his own forehead to indicate the number painted on the man's.

"All I could afford. A hundred a month's mighty steep, but worth it," he added hastily, as if criticism might offend Slocum.

"How long you been in town?"

"Got in jist 'fore the end of last month. Shoulda hung around and waited, I know, but payin' the extra money was worth it to git free of a federal marshal. When my time's up, I reckon he'll have given up on a cold trail." He reached for the number on his forehead, then drew back as if the paint might burn his fingers.

"So you get to stay until the end of October?" Slocum asked.

"Of course. I paid fer it! You ain't gonna tell Mackenzie no different."

"Settle down, partner," Slocum said. "I'm looking for a man who just blew into town in the last few days." He described Rawhide Rawlins. From the outlaw's expression, he hadn't seen Rawhide.

"Might be with the newcomers, if he didn't have 'nuff for the entire month."

"Where's that?"

Slocum realized he had crossed a line and asking a question that might bring Mackenzie and his henchmen thundering down on him. Likely, everyone in Wilson's Creek knew where the newcomers were stashed.

"Better turn in fer the night. Good night, sir." The numbered man stood and backed away, wary of Slocum shooting him in the back. In a flash he was outside the tent.

Slocum considered waylaying the man, then getting the information he needed. But how big could Wilson's Creek be? He left the tent saloon. A collective sigh of relief gusted from inside, then the gaiety he had heard before he'd entered returned. They thought he was someone he wasn't, possibly one of Mackenzie's handpicked killers.

The raucous laughter from the hotel down the street continued unabated. That had to be the head honcho's digs. Slocum veered away, cutting between tents and buildings until he reached the perimeter of the town. Again he wondered at the lack of guards. Why post them during the day but not at night?

He retrieved his horse and rode slowly around the edge of town until he saw lights some distance away, toward the hills to the west. Feeling bolder, he trotted about a mile to a deeply rutted road, then followed it toward a smaller version of the town. The namesake stream gurgled past this encampment before heading in the direction of Mackenzie's domain. Slocum slowed and looked at the arrangement of the buildings.

This looked more like a prison than most he had seen. If Rawlins wasn't in town, he had to be here. Slocum saw no way his partner in bank robbery could have avoided the guard towers on the road to the east. He wished he knew what had happened back in the canyon when Alicia had hightailed it. Had Rawlins been captured or had he bought his way into town?

He got within a hundred yards before deciding not to foolishly remain in the saddle. Again he left his gelding and crept forward on foot to scout. The sound of machinery drew him. A dozen men bent over sluices, working them back and forth as water from the stream raced down to separate gold from dross. Two men with shovels filled barrows. The men pushing the barrows disappeared on the far side.

Slocum took a deep whiff and choked. He had worked enough mines himself to recognize the pungent odor of mercury. The gold-bearing sand was treated with the mercury to form an amalgam, which was easily separated from gravel. The gold-mercury combination was then heated. The mercury fumes were captured and turned back into liquid metal while the gold was poured off into small ingots or left in pans to form pure dust. From the mercury odor and the roar of a fire blazing just out of sight inside a big building, he recognized a full-fledged mining operation.

And guards with rifles patrolled endlessly to keep the men working. Mackenzie had himself a considerable slave labor workforce.

Alicia had been right about this, at least. Slocum wondered which of those men might be her family members. Or if they toiled at the far more dangerous mercury extraction vats.

He watched long enough to know Rawhide wasn't among these men—these slaves. Slocum drifted through the buildings, hidden by heavy shadows. He found a bunkhouse filled with sleeping men and loud snores. Rawlins might be here. He started to lift the latch and enter when he heard the metallic click of a rifle being cocked behind him.

"You're a dead man if you so much as twitch toward that gun of yours," came the cold command. "Get those hands up and turn around."

Slocum did as he was told and saw he was in a worse predicament than he'd thought. Not one guard but three had caught him. He might throw down on one and hope to escape, but three? No way in hell was he going to shoot his way out of this.

8

"Put those rifles down," Slocum snapped. He began lowering his hands slowly, watching to see if the command had any effect. He had been a captain in the CSA and had learned how to make green recruits obey. It looked as if he had kept his skills ordering men around.

The guards looked from him to the man who had told him to reach for the sky, as if asking what to do. Slocum kept up the bluff.

"I was sent to find Rawlins. Mackenzie's getting antsy because this Rawlins fellow was supposed to show up an hour ago back at the hotel and didn't."

"Hotel?" The guard with the rifle still aimed at him wavered at the mention.

"You know the place," Slocum said with enough sarcasm to turn green leaves brown. "In town, at the end of the street. Two-story place with the hotel sign dangling in front of it. Headquarters?" Slocum took a shot at saying the hotel was Mackenzie's HQ. From the men coming and going, he decided this wasn't too big a risk.

"'Course I do," the guard said uneasily. The muzzle

dipped lower. If Slocum wanted, he could throw down and get at least two of the guards.

There wasn't any call for him to throw lead.

"He wants Rawlins right now. He's going to be pissed if I don't get this galoot back." He let the outlaw reach his own conclusion that anyone standing in Slocum's way was going to be in dutch with Mackenzie.

"Don't know this Rawlins. He one of the visitors?"

Slocum would have been at a loss if the guard hadn't moved unconsciously to touch his forehead. The men with numbers painted on their foreheads were called visitors. Slocum suspected they were called other things, but out of earshot. While Rawlins might have used the loot from the bank to buy his way into Wilson's Creek, Slocum took a shot in the dark that he hadn't.

"Naw, one of them." He pointed toward a line of men shuffling along with bowed heads, their legs shackled.

"What's he want with a slave?"

Slocum didn't hear what the guard farthest to his left whispered, but his partner snickered.

"Ain't no call joshin' 'bout that," the man Slocum faced said uneasily. "The thunderbird gets fed enough."

"Maybe Rawlins has already been fed to the . . . thunderbird," Slocum said, forcing himself to keep a neutral tone. The contempt he felt for anyone believing such hog wallow built inside him, but if he used it to find what he wanted without shooting it out, that was fine.

"Ain't been no one in Wilson's Creek fed to the 'bird in weeks. Heard tell a lawman out in the canyon got et, but nobody here in town."

"The 'bird can git mighty hungry in a hurry. Remember a month back?" The other two guards crowded closer. Slocum saw how they were spooked just talking about the thunderbird. They made nervous glances up at the star-packed sky as if expecting the thunderbird to swoop low on them at any instant.

"That fat peddler what thought he could call out

Mackenzie? He was warned 'bout how Mackenzie can call down the thunderbird."

"Bones. Bloody shreds of skin and gnawed bones," the third guard said, shaking his head as he remembered what was left of the peddler.

Slocum wanted to hear more about the thunderbird and if any of the men had seen it with their own eyes, but finding Rawhide mattered more.

"Mind if I check the slaves?" He pointed in the direction of the men still walking toward the dark mouth of a mineshaft.

"Won't do you no good. All them slaves been here long 'nuff fer me to learn their names. None of 'em is named Rawlins. That right, boys?" He looked over his shoulder at his two partners.

"Right, Hank. Nobody new's come onto this shift since the first of the month."

"You have any notion where I can find him? Don't want Mackenzie getting mad at me."

The three exchanged a fearful look. Slocum might have read their minds. He knew what worried them. The longer he lingered here, the more likely Mackenzie was to send out his deadly thunderbird to gobble him up—and anyone standing nearby.

"The whorehouse. If this Rawlins fella's a visitor and had his fill of that rotgut whiskey served at the saloon, he'd want to dip his wick. Plenny of ways to do that at the whorehouse."

Slocum nodded knowingly. If he asked where the cathouse was, he'd betray himself as newcomer. He had to keep the three guards thinking he was on a commission from Mackenzie.

"Thanks," he said. Slocum turned to walk back toward town, wary of where the guards' rifles pointed. None of them made a move to shoot him in the back.

He lengthened his stride and took the first chance to fade into the shadows that came along. Slocum let out a deep breath of relief. Finding that Mackenzie's henchmen feared the thunderbird so much that just mentioning it caused them to break into a sweat told him a great deal about how Mackenzie kept the town under his thumb. Reveal the thing causing such fear as a hoax and the gunmen would turn on their boss. Being made a fool of never sat well with outlaws and men used to being top gun.

Returning to town, Slocum waited impatiently outside the tent saloon. Several men, all with white numbers on their foreheads, stumbled out and pointed in several directions before deciding to head away from the hotel where Slocum thought Mackenzie lurked. Like a flock of geese, they formed a vee that spread wide enough to range them from one side of the street to the other. From their loud boasts, Slocum knew they were heading for the place he wanted.

For a moment he considered peering into the saloon again, but his notoriety from the first trip inside held him back. The last thing he wanted was a second display of marksmanship. The customers might get drunk enough to forget someone had won the barkeep's challenge. Even knee-walking drunk, they wouldn't forget a second time. He was in no mood to either fire and drill another nickel or miss. Discussion of his marksmanship either way would slow him down and increased his risks.

"Tha's the place. See the red light? Jist like Nawlins," the lead drunk said. It took a man on either side to support him all the way up the steps to the porch.

Slocum hung back and was glad he did. A bouncer came out and stopped the men. The madam didn't take kindly to rowdies, he said, but if the men wanted to set outside a spell, liquor would be served. Slocum had to admire such salesmanship. Rather than filling a soiled dove's bed, these men would be served high-priced drinks. The establishment would make as much off that *and* still have their girls active.

Pushing past into the sitting room would have drawn immediate attention from the bouncers. The working girls would have flocked over to a new customer, or maybe the madam selected the proper one for each potential patron and would keep a sharp eye out for anyone entering without being accompanied by a bouncer. Most men just off the range—or fresh from dodging a posse—didn't care a whole lot about a woman's looks. That wasn't the point of feminine companionship here. As a result, they would put up with any indignity demanded of them by the bouncers acting as gateways to the feminine delights.

He skirted the building, avoiding the bright light pouring from each window until he got to the rear of the two-story house. The back door was securely locked, probably barred inside. Even if he pulled the rickety hinge pins, the door wouldn't open enough for him to squeeze through. Making too much noise and attracting the bouncer or madam didn't enter his head. The drunks on the front porch had taken up a caterwauling song that drowned out most other sounds. When the distant coyotes began responding with their own lovelorn cries, Slocum knew no one would be paying attention to anything he did.

Seeing the drainpipe at the corner of the building, he tested it. To his surprise, it felt secure. He gingerly put his weight on it, then began climbing until he reached the eaves and swung onto the roof. It sagged more under his weight than the drainpipe, forcing him to cautiously inch along to a spot directly above an open window.

He gripped the edge of the roof, then lowered his head down enough to peer through the window. All he saw were white knees drawn up amid the bedclothes and a lusty bare-assed cowboy slamming away. Slocum straightened and got away from the window when the woman looked toward him. Even in the dim light from a coal oil lamp in the room, he saw her expression. She was bored and her eyes were bright and sharp. After her customer had finished, which seemed imminent, she would notify the bouncer of a Peeping Tom if she'd happened to spot Slocum.

He edged along the roof to the next window. The room

was deserted. Swinging down and agilely kicking at the last minute shoved his feet through onto a chair. He knocked it over and almost lost his balance. Toppling out the window to the ground twenty feet below would do him in. A quick grab on the window frame steadied him enough to recover. He slid all the way into the room, going into a crouch beside the bed. Slocum waited, heart hammering, when he heard heavy footfalls in the corridor.

His hand went to his six-gun, but he didn't draw. The door opened a few inches, stopped, then closed again. The footsteps retreated down the hallway.

Three quick strides took him to the door. He opened it and saw the bouncer's broad back vanishing down the steep stairs to the sitting room. Sounds of a new commotion told him he had a few minutes to prowl about to find Rawhide Rawlins.

Easing into the corridor, he opened the door to the room opposite. His eyes had adapted to the dark, but this room was bathed in bright light from a pair of oil lamps. He squinted and took in the room's occupant. Even with his willpower, he couldn't help calling out.

"Alicia!"

The woman sitting on the edge of the bed, head lowered, looked up with listless, defeated eyes. She turned and hiked her feet to the bed, lifting her thin shift to expose herself.

He went into the room and closed the door.

"Alicia, you—" He stared. The scantily dressed woman looked like Alicia but wasn't. Even discounting the hollow eyes and haggard expression, she was the spitting image of the woman he had met out in the canyons.

"You don't want me?"

"You look so much like Alicia Watson that it surprised me. I wasn't expecting to find her—you." Slocum cut off his flow of words. His confusion boiled over and made him seem dim-witted. There was only one reason a man came into a room like this. She expected more than surprise out of him, even if she accepted it like a slave rather than a willing partner.

"You know her? My sister?" The words came out all cracked and broken, like a mud flat dried up and curling in the hot sun.

"She's headed for a cavalry post to being back soldiers to clean out Wilson's Creek," he said.

The woman blinked but otherwise gave no response.

"You don't want me? You paid already?"

Slocum sat beside her on the bed, took her thin shoulders, and shook. For a moment the glazed expression vanished, replaced by fire such as he had seen in her sister's eyes.

"You can do that. Beat me up, but you got to pay more. Madam Catherine says so."

"Stop acting like a whore. Alicia is trying to get you and the rest of your family out of here."

"Ma and Pa? They're here? They can't see me like this." She curled up and tried to hide her nakedness with the muslin shift. All she succeeded in doing was to tear new holes in the threadbare cloth.

"Where are they? Your ma and pa?"

"Mines. Mackenzie's got them in the mines. I was lucky. He put me here."

Slocum's fury grew that the woman was so cowed that she thought being a prostitute was being lucky.

"You see a man who looked like this?" He gave a quick description of Rawhide Rawlins.

"All of 'em. None of 'em. After the first week, I didn't really see 'em anymore."

"You got clothes?" he asked. "Get dressed. We're getting out of here."

The woman pointed vaguely toward a wardrobe. Slocum yanked open the door and saw a gingham dress hanging inside. Though it was torn in places and the buttons had been ripped off the front, it covered her better than the shift. He tossed it to her. As she dressed, he asked her again, "You see a man looking like I described?"

"Heard of a man being called Rawhide," she said, settling the dress about her thin frame.

"Did he have a number painted on his forehead?"

"Might have been a visitor. Those are mostly what I get here, four, five a night. Don't mind them. Mackenzie's men like to beat me up. Once, he even watched and mocked me, making noises like the thunderbird." She shivered and hugged herself, arms tightly wrapped around her thin body.

"You ever see this thunderbird?"

"Heard it outside in the night. Saw how it killed." She shivered more.

"What's your name?"

"Loretta."

"Come on, Loretta. Let's see if we can't get your ma and pa free from the mines. I was just out there, so I know how to avoid the guards."

Slocum took her hand and pulled her along. She tried to resist, but she lacked the strength for any real fight. They went the length of the corridor to the back stairs. Looking down, Slocum saw they led into a kitchen. The back door would give them the best chance of exiting without being seen.

He pushed Loretta ahead of him. She almost fell as she missed a step on the stairs. Slocum went for his iron. Coming up the steps from the sitting room, the bouncer returned to make his rounds. A million ideas blossomed and died in Slocum's head. What would the man do when he found Loretta missing? Should Slocum gun him down if he got a chance, then make a run for it?

Rather than creating a scene sure to bring everyone in the whorehouse out to see what was happening, Slocum hurried down the stairs to the kitchen, trusting that the bouncer wouldn't discover a missing whore for at least a few minutes.

To his relief, he saw Loretta was fighting off her lethargy. The woman struggled to pull up the locking bar, but it defeated her. Slocum reached over and yanked hard, sending the wooden bar crashing into the far wall. He waited a second to see if the bouncer showed up at the head of the stairs. When no one came, he crowded behind the woman and forced her into the night. Cold air stung his cheeks and bit at his lips. He couldn't imagine how the increasingly frigid air affected Loretta, dressed only in the battered dress.

To his surprise, the cold air invigorated her rather than stealing away more of her energy.

"That way," she said, indicating the direction of the mines. "They've been there for a week." Loretta wiped at a tear, another sign that shock was wearing off. "That's more than enough time for them both to be dead."

"Let's find out," Slocum said. "If they are, their killers will pay for it."

She laughed until a touch of hysteria entered her voice.

"How do you make a thunderbird pay? You can't. That's why Mackenzie is so powerful. He controls the thunderbird."

"How?"

Loretta shrugged, then returned to her slump-shouldered stance. Slocum kept her moving at a quick pace. He had seen men during the war look like this. Defeated. Shocked from seeing too much death on the battlefield. Emotionally destroyed as their friends and brothers died around them, leaving them alive to carry on somehow. The only way to snap her out of it was to focus her attention on something positive.

"After we get your folks free, do you know how to get away from Wilson's Creek?"

She looked up. Again a flash of determination came to her eyes.

"I know how we came in. Blundered in, actually. We got separated from the others in the wagon train. Pa thought he could take a shortcut and catch up. Drove along a road 'til we saw wooden towers."

"Guard towers," Slocum said, remembering how Mackenzie's men had been stationed to protect the road.

"They greeted us like long-lost relatives. Then they stole our wagon and belongings, clapped Pa into chains, and dragged Ma off."

"How did Alicia get away?"

Loretta shook her head.

"Don't know. She was always the clever one. Mackenzie said it didn't matter that she got away, that the thunderbird would eat her. They took me to the . . . to the . . ." Her voice broke, and she began to cry.

Slocum worried that the sound would draw attention, but the night was empty. Even Mackenzie's own men feared the thunderbird, and if Loretta cried enough, it might steel her resolve to get even. He wanted to see something take hold other than resignation to the fate Mackenzie had decreed for her.

He kept her walking. Hesitantly reaching out, he put his arm around her shoulders. She shied away, and he didn't pursue her, knowing why she didn't want him—or any man—touching her.

"There's the building where I saw men sleeping," Slocum said.

"Must be another shift. Heard that Mackenzie works them twelve hours on and then twelve off."

Slocum had looked over the sleeping men and hadn't seen Rawlins. He still thought his partner had used the bank loot to buy his way into this outlaw sanctuary. Mackenzie charged for such refuge, and Slocum had no idea how long Rawhide would be safe before being driven out. He caught his breath when he realized Mackenzie wouldn't set anyone free who couldn't pay for further protection.

The clanking of chains as a new slave moved toward the mines foretold some poor soul's fate.

"Oh, my God, no!" Loretta cried.

Slocum grabbed her to prevent the woman from rushing out to the shackled prisoner shuffling along toward the gold mine.

She struggled but didn't have the strength to escape. And then Slocum saw why she had reacted.

The solitary chained prisoner was Alicia Watson.

9

"Alicia!"

Slocum clamped his hand over the girl's mouth and spun her around. They were a few yards from the bunkhouse. Any ruckus might rouse the men. Slocum hadn't seen chains holding the sleeping men, but their outcry would bring guards. He knew at least three patrolled the area around the mine. If they saw him again, this time with a whore from town, he wouldn't be able to talk his way out of getting ventilated unless he offered Loretta to them. That would set her off and betray him.

"Please, I have to help her." Loretta struggled as he picked her up and swung her about. "She'll die in the mine!"

"I know. Settle down, and I'll rescue her. You don't have to do anything but wait for us to come back."

He bodily carried her to a tool shed. Kicking open the door to reveal picks and other mining equipment, Slocum added Loretta to the pile. She fell over a wheelbarrow and tried to keep her balance. She ended up sitting in it, staring at him with wide, frightened eyes.

"Everyone who goes into the mine dies. Please let me go."

"You stay here. Don't make a fuss or the guards will come for you." He bit his lip, then knew what it would take to keep her quiet. As much as he hated saying it, he told her, "The thunderbird will hear you and carry you off."

He felt lousy seeing how this fantasy cowed her. Stepping back, he closed the door and considered barring it on the outside. Slocum knew he might get killed attempting the rescue, so he left the door unlocked. Loretta could get away if he didn't make it back. He hoped his luck held long enough that she stayed inside while he actually got to the mine or that tools weren't needed and the shed door opened by the guards.

Moving fast, he returned to the spot where they had seen Alicia being dragged along. Ore cart tracks curved around a bend and into the mine. Using piles of tailings pulled from the mine to hide his advance, he got within a few yards of the mineshaft without revealing himself to any patrolling guards.

Sounds of digging came from deep within the mine. The notion that Mackenzie forced women to work with a pick and shovel caused a hardness in Slocum that he had felt before, which always ended with someone dying. Alicia was a pretty woman, but she hadn't been as cruelly used as her sister. Until now.

Slocum made sure his six-shooter rode easy in his holster, then did the only thing he could. He squared his shoulders and moved to the ore cart tracks. As much as he wanted to run, he forced himself to walk at a steady pace to the mouth of the shaft. Miners' candles on a rock shelf at eye level gave him the way to explore deeper into the mine without worrying that he would fall down a hole. Sometimes blue dirt ran straight down and the miners tore at the floor hunting for lower ore veins.

He lit a candle and held it at arm's length as he went forward toward the sound of iron tearing at rock. The farther he got, the louder the noise became. He heard workers grunting, cursing, talking with others around them. A Y branch in the mine forced Slocum to decide which direction to go. Sounds echoed from each shaft. Flickering candlelight showed glints off an iron pick a few yards down the left tunnel.

"You," Slocum said, going to the miner with shackles on his ankles. The haggard man looked up. For a brief instant Slocum read the urge to use the pick on him, but it passed and the miner returned to his beaten look. "You see any new workers?"

"Not here," the man said.

Slocum cursed. He had chosen the wrong branch.

"Any women working in the mine?"

"Women? Not diggin'. Whole passel of 'em work at the amalgam plant out by the river."

The life of anyone working with mercury to form a gold amalgam would be pure hell, maybe worse than pulling ore from the rocky walls of this mine. But Slocum had come too far to go running off without being certain Alicia wasn't condemned to laboring underground.

"How many miners are there farther along?" Slocum pointed into the darkness. Scraping sounds told him ore was being loaded into carts to move out. "Any chance a woman might be hitched up to the ore cart to pull it out?"

"Like a donkey?" The miner laughed harshly. Again Slocum saw the man gauging his chances of getting away with a quick swing of the pick. "Naw, only men too banged up to use a pick or shovel get to pull the cart. They get to see daylight."

"It's night," Slocum said.

The miner scowled and went back to pecking away at a vein showing quartz in the dancing light from his candle.

Slocum backed off, then turned and hurried back to the fork. Less than twenty yards down the other shaft, he came to a man swinging his pick with some strength.

"You," Slocum called. "Was a woman brought in here?"

"For us? I'm married." The man turned back to his work. "Go to hell."

"As a miner," Slocum said. "Name of Alicia."

This caused the man to whirl about. He held the pickaxe with the intent of using it as a weapon.

"You think that's funny? You like tormenting me?"

"What are you talking about?"

"My daughter's name is Alicia."

"And your other's named Loretta?"

Slocum moved fast, sidestepping as the man lunged at him with the pickaxe. He tried to drive the point into Slocum's chest but missed by a wide margin when his shackles caused him to lose his balance. Slocum let him fall past to land facedown, then stepped on the pick handle to keep it flat on the ground.

"I'll rip out your heart, you bastard!"

The man threw his arms around Slocum's knees and drove him hard against the wall. Rather than drawing his six-gun and slugging the man, Slocum shoved away from the wall and drove the man back down to the ground. His knees crushed down in the middle of the struggling man's back.

"Calm down," Slocum said. "I'm trying to help."

"I'll kill you. I'll kill you all!"

Slocum grabbed a handful of shirt and pulled the man to his feet, then shoved hard and put distance between them. The fight built in the man rather than dying down.

"I promised Alicia I'd do what I could to rescue her family," Slocum said. "Loretta's hiding just outside the mine, but we saw Mackenzie's henchmen with Alicia in chains."

"You're one of them. This is some new way of tormenting me."

"You're Alicia's pa?"

"Linc Watson."

"Well, Mr. Watson, I'll see to you, too, after I get Alicia away."

"Loretta's free?"

"I got her out of the whorehouse where Mackenzie had her prisoner."

Under the dirt on his face, Linc Watson turned pale.

"He was whoring her?"

"No more. You certain Alicia wasn't brought into the mine? That means he's got her working at separating gold dust from the ore using mercury."

"She's a clever girl," Watson said. "She'll get away again."

"I ran into her east of here trying to get to a cavalry post to bring soldiers."

Watson shook his head. "They won't come. The soldiers are too afraid of—"

"The damned thunderbird," Slocum said in disgust. "What the hell is it?"

"I don't know. Mackenzie claims to control it, but there's no way he could order around an Indian spirit."

Slocum considered how hard it would be to use the pick to chop through the man's leg irons. He bent down to examine the links and locks. They had been crudely fashioned and the lock might be more easily broken than the hinge pin opposite it. Using the clumsy pickaxe would damage Watson more than his shackles.

"You're not lying? This isn't some trick? You have Loretta outside?"

"No trick. She's outside. Hunting for Alicia, too."

"My son's dead. He inhaled mercury fumes and died, but my wife's still there."

Slocum looked up at the man.

"Please, if you can't get me free, save the rest of my family. The women." Tears ran down Watson's cheeks and left tracks in the dirt. "I don't know how Loretta's going to deal with being used like that. Alicia, she's stronger. Always has been, but her sister . . ." Watson shook his head.

"That pickaxe is too dull to ever break the chains," Slocum said. "Let me go find a sledgehammer. If you put the pick edge against the chains and I hit it with a hammer . . ."

Slocum spun around on his knees and looked down the shaft to see lanterns bobbing along.

"No, no," Watson sobbed. He stumbled back, away from Slocum.

"What's goin' on there?"

Slocum reached for his six-shooter, then froze. A short, sturdy man with unnaturally powerful shoulders and arms stepped into the rocky chamber. Flanking him were gunmen with shotguns leveled. If he so much as twitched, Slocum knew he would be splattered all over the mine walls.

"I was checking this one's chains. I thought a link looked like he'd been worrying at it." He rocked back and came to his feet. If he was going to die, he'd do it on his own terms and standing tall.

"So?" The short man strutted forward. He puffed out his chest and flexed his biceps, as if this would give him the height he lacked.

Slocum got a better look at the man and knew why Watson's courage had evaporated so fast. The man's shoulders strained the fancy shirt he wore. Arms as thick as Slocum's thighs bulged and made him appear deformed. If he had been another foot taller, he would have been in proportion. But what told Slocum who he faced were the feathers adorning the man's shirt. Feathers, maybe eagle or crow, had been dyed impossibly vivid colors. Reds and blues and a yellow with purple highlights swayed every time the man moved.

The man pointed. His huge hands were gnarled and looked as if a cougar had chewed on them, leaving behind raw meat. A slender waist and legs so tiny they might have belonged to a youngster completed the picture. Almost.

Slocum looked into the dark eyes and saw a bottomless pit of loco.

"So, Mr. Mackenzie," Slocum said, guessing the man's identity, "the chains are nice and secure. No way is he going to get free."

Mackenzie made a cackling sound and bobbed up and down the way a chicken would before pecking at grains of corn. The gunman on his right came forward, slugged

Watson in the gut with the butt of his shotgun, and then looked at the chains.

"Look good to me, Mr. Mackenzie."

"Good to know a guard's on the ball. Can't turn your back on these sons of bitches in the mines, not for an instant." Mackenzie spun about and bent forward, presenting his cracker ass and making cawing sounds. He spun about and clawed at the air with his gnarled hands. "You come with us. We're going back to the nest."

Watson turned his face away. More tears streamed down his cheeks. Slocum couldn't tell if the man avoided a direct glance so he wouldn't give away his possible benefactor or thought Slocum had been lying. If it hadn't been for the attentiveness of Mackenzie's bodyguards, Slocum would have shown the prisoner some leaden truth. As it was, he followed Mackenzie out, the man bobbing and dancing to music only he heard. All the way out into the night, Slocum felt the presence of the shotguns pointed at his spine.

Mackenzie couldn't know every man in his employ. Or was he cagier than that? If he knew Slocum was an interloper, why not have the guards just gun him down?

When they reached the open air, Mackenzie threw back his head and turned his face to the sky. A screech like a hoot owl erupted from his lips. As quickly as it started, he cut it off.

"That's to appease the thunderbird," Mackenzie said in a tone so normal as to be frightening. "Don't want to get on its bad side. It's a powerful spirit, the thunderbird."

"Surely is, sir," both guards said in unison.

Slocum felt obligated to chime in, so he said, "Never cross an Indian spirit bird."

Mackenzie looked hard at him. A bent finger stabbed him in the chest.

"You're right." With that, he dashed off, laughing crazily.

"Come on. We gotta keep up. Don't want the boss kept

waitin'." The man behind Slocum nudged him with the shotgun.

"What about the men in the mine?" Slocum said. "I was supposed to guard them."

"Don't worry. The thunderbird will eat 'em all up if they try to escape."

"Yeah," said the second guard. "Bein' outside at night's a death sentence 'cuz that's when the thunderbird hunts. Good thing we're with the boss. Only he can control it."

"Or call it down from the sky," finished the first guard.

Both men laughed and started running. Slocum paused, considering his chances and realizing they weren't good. He lit out after them, looking around, hoping to catch sight of Loretta. Though they ran past the shed where he had left her, he didn't see the woman. And nowhere did he catch sight of Alicia. As her pa had said, she must have been taken to the amalgam plant fifty yards away, near the rapidly running namesake for the town.

Either the two gunmen were slower than him or they slowed to let him catch up. Slocum found himself flanked by them as they returned to town.

Panting harshly, one gasped out, "Ain't seen you here before. You jist git to town?"

"Just did," Slocum said. "How long you been here?"

"Since the boss recruited me over in Halliday. I got cross with the law and was gonna hang fer murderin' some lily liver what wouldn't apologize fer callin' me a half-breed. I ain't no breed. My folks was both from Italy."

"Busted you out of Hillstrom's jail?" Slocum asked.

"You been there, too?" The man's sudden interest told Slocum he had said the wrong thing.

"The marshal came for me. Warrants from three counties. I got out of town ahead of a posse."

"Warrants fer what?"

"I killed three men who asked too many questions," Slocum said as coldly as he could. He didn't want friends. The two with him would gun him down on a whim—or at Mackenzie's order. He didn't want to hesitate an instant if he had to kill them to protect himself.

Thinking on how these men likely had their way with Loretta and had sent the rest of Watson's family to the gold mines as slaves to die working for a crazy bastard helped that along.

"Gotta slow down," gasped the man on his left. "Lungs are on fire."

"Don't pant too much," said the other. "That sounds like a dyin' animal. The thunderbird will come for you if it thinks you're dyin'."

The men sounded too sincere to be joshing him. Whenever a new cowboy signed on to an outfit, the old wranglers told outrageous stories to scare him. Slocum had done it himself. But he didn't hear the joking with these two. They believed what they said about the thunderbird, just as Alicia Watson had.

"There," panted one. "The boss is already there. How the little turd runs so fast on them bandy legs is a mystery."

Slocum saw the lance of orange flame almost at the same time as the complaining guard gasped, stood upright, then twisted and collapsed.

On the hotel's front porch, Mackenzie stood with a rifle pulled snugly to his shoulder. He levered in another round and pointed it smack at Slocum.

10

"He didn't mean nuthin' by it, Mr. Mackenzie," the guard to Slocum's right sputtered. "He was just funnin' . . . and I never agreed with him, no sir, never did."

Slocum saw that Mackenzie's rifle remained trained on him, not the blubbering fool beside him. Mackenzie stood partially hidden in shadow, with the bright lights from inside the hotel spilling out beside the man. If he moved even a foot closer, he would be outlined so Slocum could get a good shot. The range favored the rifle, but Slocum knew he didn't have a chance otherwise.

"Now, tell me why I shouldn't just feed both you boys to the 'bird?"

"You'd lose two good men," Slocum replied calmly.

"I been here fer a whole month, sir. I done ever'thing you ast. I—"

Mackenzie swung his rifle and fired. Whether he was a crack shot or damned lucky didn't matter to the man catching the slug in the middle of his face. He went down as surely as his partner.

"Can't stand a man who whines," Mackenzie said. He did

a tiny dance, then jumped and clicked his heels. Feathers fluttered down all around him as if he'd molted. When he lit back down with a sharp snap on the wood planking, he had the rifle aimed once more at Slocum. "You don't whine, do you?"

Slocum said nothing. This appealed to the ruler of Wilson's Creek. He lowered his rifle and waved one of his powerful arms for Slocum to come closer. As if walking amid newborn kittens, Slocum took several steps until Mackenzie was limned by the lamplight spilling from inside.

"You arm wrestle?"

The question took Slocum by surprise. He nodded and said, "Won a bet or two that way."

"Come on inside. Let's arm wrestle."

Mackenzie beat Slocum into the hotel lobby by half a minute.

The short man had already pushed up his sleeve to reveal his powerful biceps and had his elbow planted on a table.

"Come on, let's arm wrestle. You lose, you buy me a drink."

"What if I win?" Slocum asked.

Anger flashed across Mackenzie's face and madness danced in his eyes, then he said in a perfectly level voice, "Not going to happen."

From the way his arm and shoulder muscles rippled, Slocum considered that likely. He sat, planted his elbow on the table, and worked over possible tactics. Even if he proved stronger—or cagier since arm wrestling was as much about leverage and grip as strength—should he lose?

Mackenzie almost pinned him outright, his thick hand and bent fingers leaping out and engulfing Slocum's. Only a loud cry and incredible luck saved Slocum from immediate defeat. He shifted slightly and got a better grip, which allowed him to push Mackenzie's arm back to upright. Now Mackenzie's henchmen started catcalling and cheering on their boss.

Slocum gritted his teeth and tried to move the man's arm.

Mackenzie budged a half inch. Then an inch. Slocum's back began aching from the strain. He thought every muscle in his arm would explode from the effort, but he pushed Mackenzie's hand down another inch. Only three or four to go.

Then it was as if he'd been shoved against a brick wall. Even rising in the chair and unfairly using his body weight failed to gain him an advantage.

With a cry of triumph, Mackenzie heaved and slammed Slocum's hand hard against the table. He held it there, crushing down until Slocum winced. He refused to cry out even if it meant breaking his gun hand. Just when Slocum was sure Mackenzie would rip off important body parts, the man relented.

Slocum rubbed his arm to get circulation back into it.

"I win," Mackenzie crowed.

"You did, sir," Slocum said, the words ash on his tongue.

"You owe me a drink. Go fetch it."

Slocum stood and almost cried out in pain. Across his back and shoulders and all the way down his right arm burned as if he had thrust them into a blacksmith's forge. He shook his hand and flexed it. Nothing broken, but he found it hard to close his hand into a fist. The muscles simply wouldn't obey.

He went to the bar and wondered how the hell he would pay for a drink. He was flat broke. Whatever money he had counted on had been snatched away by Rawhide Rawlins.

"Here," the woman behind the bar said, sliding a shot of some green liquor across it to him. She moved so Slocum's body blocked Mackenzie's view and pulled a gold coin from her ample cleavage. Then acting as if he'd just given it to her, she held the coin up so her boss and the others in the room could see it.

"Thanks, mister," she said, then turned and tossed the coin into a cup with a loud ring.

"I owe you one," Slocum whispered, and smiled.

"Get me out of here the way you did Loretta and we're more than even," she whispered back.

Slocum hesitated. He hadn't thought anyone saw him rescuing Loretta Watson.

"There's not much in Wilson's Creek that doesn't get seen by somebody," the woman said in a low voice. She pushed back a strand of coppery hair and her green eyes fixed on Slocum's. "Be glad it was me spying on you and not one of them owlhoots."

He turned with the drink balanced on his right palm, and holding it with his left to keep it from spilling. He heard the woman say behind him, "I'm Erika. Don't forget me."

He returned to Mackenzie's table and set the drink down gingerly.

"To the winner!" Slocum managed to raise his right arm to lead the others in three cheers.

Mackenzie beamed at the attention. Slocum considered his chances for dragging out his smoke wagon and removing this muscled freak from the face of the earth. He might get some help from Erika and maybe a couple of the men in the room. That was all it would take, if he could only wrap his fingers around the ebony handle of his Colt Navy.

If only.

"Great drink," Mackenzie said, running a thick finger around the rim of the empty glass to snare the last drop. He lifted it to his lips as he appraised Slocum. "You've done good. Get on back to the mine and keep those lazy bastards working."

"Right away," Slocum said. He headed for the door, wondering if Mackenzie would shoot him in the back. Instead the man said something that quieted the low murmur from the others in the room.

"Don't let the thunderbird get you." Mackenzie's cruel laughter followed Slocum out of the hotel and partway to the mines.

In spite of himself, he looked over his shoulder at the empty sky. No moon, no clouds, only sharp, hard points of stars. But if there had been the slightest hint of a bird diving on him, Slocum knew his heart would have exploded.

He walked a little faster, damning Mackenzie for planting the idea that the thunderbird existed. It was only the way the man kept the others in line, what with his fake feathers sewed onto his shirt and hideous cawing and curious birdlike movements. Slocum couldn't tell if the man was crazy as shit or using his brain to keep the town under his thumb. If Mackenzie was smart, Slocum had to worry more than if he was crazy. Sane, the man might be playing with him in a way a loco hombre never could.

Whatever the state of the man's sanity, he was dangerous.

By the time Slocum reached the mine, he had rubbed the soreness from his right arm and could close his right hand, though his grip remained weak. He started into the mine, but the three guards he had run into before arrayed themselves across the mouth. Even if he broke Linc Watson free of his chains, there wasn't any way they could sneak out past the guards.

Slocum veered away toward the shed where he had left Loretta, only to keep walking when one of the guards saw him and waved. To talk to her now would cause problems he didn't want to solve. Instead, he waved back and went to the amalgam plant, where bright fumes rose from a boiler, curling into the crisp nighttime air.

If he couldn't get Watson free, he could find his wife and get her and her daughter to safety.

He pressed his back against a brick wall and looked around for guards. The distant horizon glowed with the promise of dawn. Slocum knew he had to hurry. Walking around with two women, neither in chains, would draw attention in Mackenzie's town.

Edging along the wall, he chanced a quick look into the

building. If a door had ever been hung there, it was long gone along with its hinges and part of the frame. Slocum drew his pistol and stepped into the room where a half-dozen men and women worked with pans, rolling beads of mercury around in rock dust taken from crushed ore. When they accumulated enough gold in the bright beads, they tipped the pan and let the mercury-gold amalgam roll off into a trough. At the far end of the trough two men worked to get the mercury into a vat, where it was heated. One man stoked the fire under the vat and the other scraped the gold left behind into a sack.

It didn't surprise Slocum to see an armed guard standing behind the man with the bag of gold dust. It wouldn't be much of a stretch to imagine the man skimming dust from the sack for his own use before taking it to Mackenzie. As that thought hit Slocum, he considered demanding to carry the current bag to Mackenzie and seeing what the reaction was. Revealing the number of guards here would help get Alicia's mother free.

Even identifying her would be hard since there were a dozen withered women here, too used up for even a whorehouse. One moved with a crippled leg. Another cackled as she pushed the mercury around in the pan in front of her. Slocum had seen how quickly mercury fumes addled brains when he worked at a mill in California. He had been responsible for crushing the ore, not the separation of gold from dross.

Mackenzie took the gold, but the dross here was all human.

Coughing from the fumes drew attention to him. The guard watching the gold dust being raked off to the bag looked up. Then he pointed his rifle in Slocum's direction, not aiming but alert.

"What you want?" the guard called.

"Came for one of the workers," Slocum said. "Name of Watson. The boss wants to see her."

"Back there. She's the one working on the ledger."

Slocum nodded, as much to acknowledge the information as to hide his face. He wanted to spirit Mrs. Watson away without gunfire. Dead bodies drew unwanted attention. More than this, Slocum doubted the guard stood watch alone. There had to be someone watching him.

He made his way through the equipment strewn around. Containers of mercury heavier than Slocum could pick up alone made him wonder if Mackenzie had once lugged such bottles around. The man was immensely strong, and being near the mercury too long would discombobulate him.

A woman bent over a table, pen in hand as she worked on a ledger, caught his attention. Slocum ducked into the room. The woman's gray hair hung in dirty strings. A bit of drool trickled from the corner of her mouth to the desktop. She never noticed as she toiled to move figures from scraps of paper to the ledger.

"Mrs. Watson? Your husband told me you were here." He waited for a response that would confirm she was the woman he sought.

"Linc? Where is he?" She looked around. Her bloodshot eyes failed to focus properly.

"I'll take you to Loretta. Your daughter. And then I'll see to getting Alicia out of here, too."

"My girls?" This perked her up. Then she slumped. "My boy died. The thunderbird killed him." She wiped her mouth with her sleeve, then turned back to her work lining up numbers for Mackenzie.

Even if Mackenzie was as crazy as a loon, he wanted an accounting of the gold taken from the mine. Slocum wished he could take the ledger with him to turn over to the law as evidence of what Mackenzie did here. Then he realized how dangerous that would be for him, a bank robber. More than this, dealing with the Watson women required his full attention.

He flexed his hand again. It still ached and lacked

strength, but it was close enough to normal for him to have
confidence in his gun-handling abilities.

"How many guards are here?"

"Two. He pays them well." She began leafing through the
ledger and stopped at a page with names and amounts. Her
finger stabbed down. "See? A hundred dollars a month. And
sanctuary. That's worth another hundred a month."

Slocum didn't know how much they had taken from the
Halliday bank, but it had to be enough for Rawlins to buy
at least a few months' asylum from Mackenzie.

He walked around the woman and examined her chains.
These were simpler than the irons used on the miners.
Instead of a lock, a simple rivet had been used to hold shut
the shackles. Breaking the links did nothing to relieve the
weight of the heavy iron clamps around her ankle. He looked
around and found a discarded iron rod in the corner, dropped
to the floor, and inserted the shaft between the flanges on
her shackle. With a jerk, he popped the rivet holding it to
her flesh.

The shackle and chain clattered to the floor. Slocum
peered around the table to see if the noise had alerted either
of the guards. He knew one hovered near the gold dust. The
other might be asleep or prowling about, checking solitary
workers like Mrs. Watson. He waited a full minute, then
stood and took the woman by the arm.

"We're leaving now."

"My work's not done." She tried to grab her ledger.

"He wants you to see your daughter. Loretta. And do you
know where Alicia is?"

"Alicia's always been a handful. Willful, feisty. Full of
piss and vinegar." She stared at him, eyes wide. "Shouldn't
say things like that. Linc doesn't like it when I do."

"I'll get you and your girls together, then you can ask
your husband to forgive you." He gripped her arm and
steered her to the door. There, he decided stealth gained him

nothing and openness did. He waved to the gold dust guard and called, "Thanks. Got her. See you at the, uh, nest."

He shoved her along because Mrs. Watson wanted to return for her ledger book. One errant comment and she would bring down a hail of bullets. In the main room Slocum again felt woozy from the fumes rising from the amalgam tables and the vat where the mercury was cooked off.

Slocum kept her stumbling along, her gait uncertain, and into the first light of dawn. Barely had they left the amalgam separation factory when Slocum saw the three mine guards coming straight for them.

He moved behind her to hide how he drew his six-shooter in preparation for a gunfight. Only, his injured hand betrayed him. The Colt slid from his grip and landed in the dirt.

The guards yelled and ran for him.

11

Mrs. Watson swung about, her elbow catching Slocum on the side of his head as he knelt to retrieve his six-gun. The blow knocked him to the ground. He rolled and went for his gun but froze when he saw a guard with his rifle trained on him. The woman let out a shriek and ran off. Slocum was momentarily blinded by the rising sun as she vanished to the east.

"What the hell happened?" The guard circled Slocum, ready to shoot.

Slocum's mind raced.

"Put that rifle down, you idiot," he snapped. "Mackenzie wanted her. I was taking her to him when she saw you and bolted."

"Cole and Lex will get her," the guard said. "How'd you let her get away? You know you're supposed to leave them slaves all chained up anytime we're walkin' 'em from here to there."

Slocum saw the man was more inclined to ask questions than shoot. He took the chance of picking up his six-shooter. His fingers curled about the handle, but his full strength hadn't returned yet.

"I arm wrestled Mackenzie. My hand's not back to what it was. Had my gun out to cover her when you spooked her. She caught me in the face with her elbow, then lit out."

Slocum holstered his Colt, got to his feet, and brushed himself off. He held out his hand and flexed it.

"Mackenzie beat me as easy as any man could," he said, knowing the guard was well aware of that.

"You had to buy him one of them twenty-dollar drinks he swills, eh? You stupid bastard."

"How could I tell him to piss up a rope? He's the boss," Slocum said.

"Last month, he fed a new guy to the thunderbird for refusin' to arm wrestle. You done right, but he'll cut you into small pieces to feed to the 'bird if they don't run her down." The guard looked after his partners. "You got the luck of the Irish with you. Cole caught her."

Slocum considered what to do. The two guards marched a babbling Mrs. Watson back. All she could say had to do with her ledger. If he thanked the men and tried to get away with her, he bought himself a passel of trouble. This was especially true if the guards, now off duty, insisted on accompanying him and his prisoner back to the hotel. Mackenzie wouldn't buy any of his lies. From her addled condition, Mrs. Watson might even blurt out what he'd said about her daughters.

"You want us to take her to Mackenzie?" The one named Cole prodded the woman in the back with his rifle.

"I'd better ask. Get her fastened down to her table," Slocum said, hating to leave Mrs. Watson in chains but seeing no other way out of his predicament. If he got himself killed, her husband, Loretta, Alicia, and she would all die in Wilson's Creek. Staying free of chains himself was the best he could do for her now. "I'll ask Mackenzie what to do."

"You be careful 'bout that, boy," said Lex, an older man with a dour expression. "He don't like it when his men, especially greenhorns, can't carry out his orders."

"Thanks for the advice. It's for the good if you don't spread this around. I'll buy you all drinks later to thank you." Slocum saw the promise of free whiskey in exchange for a few hours' silence appealed to the men.

Slocum had to wonder about the one guard claiming that the green liquor Mackenzie drank cost twenty dollars a shot. If that was the going price, he owed the barkeep, Erika, his life.

He didn't have twenty cents in his pocket, much less twenty dollars. Mackenzie didn't seem the type of man to go easy on a welsher, even if Slocum hadn't known what he was getting himself into with the bet.

Slocum waited until the guards dragged Mrs. Watson back into the amalgam works before cutting off at an angle to the shed where he had left Loretta. The bad luck that had bedeviled him rescuing the Watson family could only get worse if she had hightailed it. He jerked open the door, expecting to find her gone. To his surprise, she had curled up on some burlap bags and was snoring softly.

He ducked inside and pulled the door shut behind him. The noise brought her awake and screaming. He clamped his hand over her mouth.

"It's me, Slocum. We're getting out of here now."

"Out?"

"Out of Wilson's Creek. I don't know where I can stash you while I find your sister, but I know where your ma and pa are."

"Alicia?"

"She's around town somewhere."

"I saw her. While you were gone. A man led her toward the hotel. Where Mackenzie stays. What he calls his nest. She was all chained up."

Slocum's mind raced. It would be safer getting Loretta out, then returning for Alicia, but he felt as if his luck was wearing thin. The guards all accepted him as one of their own, and even Mackenzie didn't question him being in

Wilson's Creek. That had to end eventually. He had almost revealed himself trying to get Mrs. Watson free.

"You sure about that?"

"To the hotel," Loretta said.

"I want you to stay here. Hide the best you can." He worried that the miners would come for new picks or other equipment stored in the shed.

"You're going to save her?"

"Help me move some of the tools outside." Slocum grabbed shovels and picks and dumped them outside the shed. Anyone coming for equipment wouldn't have to open the shed for it now. "I don't know how long I'll be."

"Why are you helping us? I don't know you."

"I promised your sister."

Loretta stared at him with wide, almost childlike eyes.

"You keep your word," she said as if this settled everything.

In Slocum's mind, it did. He had promised.

Making sure she closed the shed door, Slocum walked back into town. The likeliest place for Alicia to have been taken loomed at the end of the street. Mackenzie's headquarters. The hotel. The nest.

Walking to the rear, he rattled locked doors and tried windows until he found one that creaked open far enough for him to slide through. He landed inside a dusty room littered with old rags and carrying the pungent smell of bleach. A quick look out the door into a back hallway failed to reveal any guards. He stepped out, dusted himself off, and worried the bleach odor clinging to his clothes might draw attention. There was no cure for this. He went exploring.

Ten guards in the lobby sprawled on sofas and chairs, all asleep. The stairs leading to the second floor beckoned to him with a Siren's call when he heard Mackenzie's voice from above.

"So, my dear, it is time for you to be educated."

Slocum couldn't make out Alicia's answer, but he

recognized her voice. He walked on cat's feet across the lobby and climbed the steep stairs to the top floor. A quick check of the first room revealed nothing. The second room puzzled him. Books stacked in floor-to-waist-high piles threatened to topple over. Mechanical gadgets lay about the room, pipes and coils of wire and even rolls of cloth. None of it made any sense to Slocum.

He heard Mackenzie droning on, reading something. Slocum went to the far end of the hallway and pressed his ear against the door panel. Alicia mumbled and a chain clanked. Slocum went in fast, six-shooter drawn and ready to fire a slug into Mackenzie's crazy brain.

Alicia struggled on the bed, a gag in her mouth. Chains held her firmly in place, but her clothing, while filthy, hadn't been badly ripped to show that any unwanted sexual congress had already occurred. She twisted and inclined her head. Slocum spun about, finger tightening on the trigger. He faced an open window.

She thrashed about and made noises, which he ignored as he looked out the window for any sign of Mackenzie. The man was nowhere to be seen. From dusty footprints on a ledge along the eaves of the roof, he had escaped this way. But no matter how far out Slocum leaned, he couldn't catch sight of him.

Not wanting to waste any more time, he ducked back and went to Alicia. From the way she continued to fight and rant, he considered leaving the gag in her mouth.

"Stay quiet or you'll have all his henchmen down on our necks." As she quieted, he unfastened the gag. She started to complain. He clamped his hand over her mouth and shook his head. "Be quiet."

Slocum almost laughed. The Watson women were hard to shut up. He had done the same thing with Loretta.

"What's so funny? You're smiling?"

"I need to get you out of the chains." He examined the shackles. Like those that held her mother, they weren't difficult to break, but he needed tools. "Wait here."

"John, come back!"

He hurried to the room where he had seen all the books and strange contraptions. Kicking through piles on the floor, he found a chisel and hammer. Somehow, he had the feeling of being watched although a quick look around the room failed to reveal any spying eyes. Still, Mackenzie had gone somewhere and had disappeared fast. The window to this room was open, too.

Slocum frowned. Had it been open the first time he'd come in? He couldn't remember.

Retreating to the back of the hotel, he went to Alicia, positioned the chisel, and took a hard whack. The rivet popped from the iron cuff on her right leg.

"Oh, that feels good," she sobbed out. "Hurry. Get me out of the rest."

Slocum made quick work of the other leg shackle and those on her wrists. She rubbed vigorously. Her fingers came away bloody from the abrasions.

"I got your sister free."

"Loretta! What about Ma and Pa?"

"Later. Your ma's in a bad way. You'll have to take care of her."

"They caught me right after dawn, after I left you. It was like they were waiting." She glared at him. "You didn't sell me out to Mackenzie, did you?"

"No reason to do that. I'm hunting for my friend."

"I thought you might have swapped me for him."

"We have to get out of here. Mackenzie might come back."

"He . . . I don't know. He didn't try to rape me. He read to me from some Italian book about a man called Da Vinci. I didn't understand it and said so. That's when he gagged me."

"I'll gag you if you don't shut up." Slocum pushed her behind him as they descended the stairs. "Not a word till we're away."

He considered retreating the way he had entered the

hotel, but a more direct exit presented itself. Leading the way, he went directly to the front door and opened it. On the hotel veranda several more of Mackenzie's gang slept. He shot Alicia a warning look when she gasped.

Cavorting about in the street in front of the hotel, Mackenzie flapped his arms and made loud cawing sounds. Slocum slipped his Colt from the holster but Mackenzie ducked and bobbed about like an Indian doing a war dance. In a flash, he had run down the street and vanished along a side street.

Indecision hit Slocum. Mackenzie couldn't have gone far. Killing him would make everything in Wilson's Creek fall apart. Cut the head off the rattlesnake, and even if it didn't die until sundown, it was still dead. The noises the tail made wouldn't amount to anything more than dying convulsions.

"You have to get us out, John," Alicia said. "Please."

That made sense to him. He jammed his six-shooter back into his cross-draw holster and pointed toward the edge of town where he had left his horse.

"Is she there? Loretta?"

"We need horses for both of you. Mine won't carry three of us."

Getting the horses proved too easy. Outside the general store they found two horses saddled and patiently waiting. Slocum knew there'd be an uproar when the owners came out and the horses were missing. That added urgency to an already desperate need to get the hell out of town.

He swung onto one as Alicia mounted the other. They galloped off to the spot where Slocum had tethered his horse. He vaulted over, glad to settle down in a saddle worn down to fit his butt.

"Where is she?"

"You stay here. I'll get her," Slocum said. He grabbed the spare horse's reins and knew before he had gone a dozen yards that Alicia wasn't obeying. "Get back," he called, then relented.

Arguing now only stole away precious time. Mackenzie would return and see that Alicia had flown the coop or the owners of the two horses would raise a hue and cry. With the sun edging up over the mountains, the entire town would come alive soon enough and make escape impossible.

Galloping in an arc to avoid as much of the town as possible, Slocum finally set a route straight for the mine. If the guards accosted him, they would die. But finally luck smiled on him. The day shift had gone into the mines to keep their minions at work. The guards overseeing the amalgam plant were nowhere to be seen. For a moment, Slocum considered trying to free Mrs. Watson again, then knew getting the daughters to safety counted more. The older woman might be permanently addled from the mercury, but there was still hope for Loretta. And Alicia hadn't been subjected to any of that abuse.

He hit the ground running and crashed into the side of the shed.

"Loretta, time to go. I've got a horse." His heart caught in his throat. No answer. "Loretta?"

"Please, Lo, we have to go. Now!" Alicia cried.

Her sister's voice lured the frightened woman out. A scraping sound meant a locking bar was removed. The door opened a crack, then Loretta rushed out and clung to her sister's leg.

"Up. There's time for that later." Slocum caught Loretta around her trim waist and lifted her bodily onto the stolen horse. "No talking until we get past the guard towers."

He galloped off, sure they would trail behind. As he approached the road leading into the canyon and escape, he saw the tower guards marching out, heads down as if they were the prisoners and not in charge. The other fortified spots remained unmanned. He judged distances and decided he didn't have to decoy the guards away from the two women. That would end his credibility with anyone in Wilson's Creek, but it wouldn't matter. They would all be free.

"Th-They're climbing into the towers," gasped out Alicia. "Ride faster."

"John, please, Lo is having a hard time. She's so weak!"

"Ride!"

The bend in the canyon finally blocked the view of any tower guard. Only then did he slow and let the Watson girls catch up with him. Again he marveled at how much they looked alike. They might have been mistaken for twins at one time, but not now. Loretta was drawn, pale, and emaciated. Alicia still retained a vitality that pleased Slocum. Still, seeing them side by side made it obvious they were sisters.

"We have to go farther than I did before. I didn't want to leave you, John, but I wasn't going back to Wilson's Creek. I wanted to get the cavalry."

"Mackenzie's gang caught you."

Alicia nodded sadly. "They must patrol the entire area. There were four of them. They boxed me in, and I had no place to run."

"I tried to find my friend but never did."

"In Wilson's Creek? I saw several newcomers," she said.

"Quiet!" Slocum cocked his head to one side and listened hard. "Riders, coming from town. Not fast but making good time." He looked around. The only way to escape lay down the canyon, away from town.

"Up there, John. In the rocks!" Alicia had spotted a dark oval that hinted at a cave.

"If it's not deep enough to hide the horses, we're goners." He saw that Loretta might not make it much farther. Even on horseback for such a short time, she wobbled and looked ready to keel over at any instant.

He silently led the way. They had to take the chance the cave would hold them and the horses so that Mackenzie's guards missed them.

Picking the way through a tumble of rocks took longer than he had hoped, but they still reached the cave. To his relief it had a tall, narrow opening with a larger room just past. He dismounted and led his horse in. When he was satisfied the horse wasn't going to get spooked, he helped Alicia with her sister and her horse. Alicia crowded in with her horse seconds later.

"Stay here," Slocum said, going back to scout the outlaws after them.

The six men weren't hurrying but kept a steady pace. Slocum caught his breath as the gang passed where Slocum and the Watson girls had left the trail. No one even glanced down to see the trail leading to the cave. But two men falling back from the others irked Slocum. Strung out, they might be taking posts along the trail.

He eased back into the cave.

"They went by," he told Alicia. He looked down and saw how Loretta had curled up in a tight ball and already slept heavily.

"She's exhausted. I've never seen her look so . . . so drained, physically or emotionally."

"Let her sleep. We ought to also, since the guards are likely to be out there all day."

"They never go out at night," Alicia said.

"The thunderbird," Slocum said. For once he appreciated how the superstition would help them. As soon as the guards returned to Wilson's Creek for the night, they could leave and put a considerable number of miles between them and Mackenzie.

"I hadn't realized it, but I am tired, too," Alicia said. "You look worn out, as well."

Slocum had been running on pure determination. He was hungry and tired. The sleep would do him good, but he shook his head.

"Somebody's got to stand watch."

"Why? If they find us in here, they've got us trapped. The only way back to the canyon floor is that narrow trail.

Sleep, John. Come on." Alicia settled on the dirty floor and held out her arms.

He sank beside her and soon they lay together, arms wrapped around the other, sleeping heavily.

The next thing Slocum knew, he came awake with his six-gun in his grip when a hideous cry rang out. He sat up, saw Loretta was missing, then pushed to his feet. It was pitch black in the cave. He had slept away the day.

"Lo," Alicia called. "Where are you?"

Slocum let Alicia hunt around inside the cave for her wayward sister. He went outside. It was dusk going into night, but he made out the body on the ground a few yards away.

Loretta Watson had been ripped to shreds.

12

"Lo! Loretta!"

Slocum grabbed Alicia before she could rush to her sister's body. She fought and then collapsed, sinking to her knees, sobbing. He made certain she wasn't going to leave the mouth of the cave before he edged forward, six-gun ready.

He didn't pay any attention to Loretta. She was obviously dead. Rather, Slocum kept a sharp eye above. The rocks over the cave didn't reveal any predators. Listening revealed small scraping sounds farther downhill, back in the direction of the canyon floor. Slocum stepped over the bloody corpse and jumped to the top of a rock to get a better view of the terrain.

Shadows moved about, but he had no target. The dusk hardened into night, denying him any chance of seeing what had clawed Loretta so brutally to death. He slid off the rock and holstered his pistol. The immediate danger was gone. But where had the predator come from to kill the woman? A quick examination of the rocky ground around the body showed nothing, but Slocum hadn't expected to find anything. There hadn't been any useful prints near Dupree either.

"The thunderbird," sobbed Alicia. "It comes out at night and got Loretta. It took her. It *ate* her!"

He shook her so hard her head snapped back. She looked up at him but her eyes were focused a thousand yards away.

"There's no such thing. I don't know what's going on, but there's no Indian spirit killing people."

"It comes out of storms, at night, when—"

"There's no such thing," he repeated, shaking her even harder to make certain she got the point. "Mackenzie is responsible for this. He's playing with us. He's crazy and enjoys pretending there's a thunderbird." Slocum was sure Mackenzie used fear and superstition to keep his gunmen in line and cow the slaves and paid visitors to Wilson's Creek. "We'll get out of these damned canyons."

"My ma and pa. You've got to rescue them," she said. "If Mackenzie is doing this—or commanding the thunderbird to do his killing—he knows I'm gone. He'll take revenge on my family."

Slocum wanted to find Rawhide Rawlins but wasn't going to risk his life needlessly to rescue the man or get back the stolen money.

"You were right before," Slocum said. "Get the cavalry and ferret out Mackenzie. That's what you need to do."

"Now, John, you have to get my family out of there *now*."

"We—"

"I know where Rawlins is. You'll never find him if I don't tell you."

He looked at her. Tears stained her cheeks, but her mouth had become a razor's slash with determination, and the set of her chin showed she meant it.

"Too dangerous. He's probably paid for his own safety in the town."

"He hasn't. I know where he is. Get Ma and Pa out and

I'll tell you. I give you my word—on my sister's grave, I promise."

If Rawlins hadn't paid his way into town, that meant he was working as a slave. Slocum had always liked Rawhide but knew the lure of money changed men mighty fast. Still, things had been confused when Lee Dupree had died, and Slocum had no real proof that Rawhide had gone willingly to Wilson's Creek. Mackenzie's roving patrol might have snared him, stolen the bank loot, then taken him to town to work until he died.

Or they might have killed him out of hand after stealing the money. Finding the man's body if they hid it along the trail into Wilson's Creek would be impossible.

But why should they hide the body? Slocum felt his head begin to hurt from too much thinking. It was time to act.

"You'd lie to get your family free," he said, watching her reaction.

"Of course I would. But I'm not lying, and I'm not bargaining. Get them free and I'll tell you where your friend is."

"You weren't in town long enough," he said.

She got into a staring match with him that convinced him of what he had to do.

"The ground's too hard to bury your sister," he said.

"We'll pile rocks. A cairn. It's not much but it'll have to be enough."

Slocum hadn't expected her to help, but Alicia did. An hour later, her sister's body had been covered with a hundred pounds of rocks placed as carefully as possible to keep the animals from dining off the corpse. He finally stepped back and wiped his hands on his jeans.

"I'll say a few words," Alicia said.

Slocum stepped back and let her pray. He looked into the night sky when he heard a soft whooshing sound. For a moment he thought he saw a bird gliding across the stars, blocking their bright, hard points, but the shadow vanished. By the time he relaxed, Alicia had finished.

"You go right on back while the guards are out of the towers. They fear the thunderbird and won't return until daybreak."

"Where's Rawlins? I can get him when I get your parents."

"He—no, John. You're an honorable man but temptation might get the better of you. You find your friend and where's the incentive to bother with my parents? There are a hundred excuses you could make for not rescuing them."

He wouldn't do that, and she knew it. But Slocum had to face reality. Getting Alicia's ma and pa out of Wilson's Creek would be hard. With a third prisoner to save, getting away became even harder. What she asked of him was logical, but it put him in great danger. Mackenzie was on the lookout now after losing both Watson girls as prisoners. If the parents were successfully spirited away, Slocum had to return for Rawhide Rawlins. A third escape attempt took on impossibly high chances of failure.

The only good thing for Slocum and Rawhide lay in the fact that they could leave town and go wherever they wanted. Alicia and her family would be on the trail away from Wilson's Creek, riding to the cavalry post. By the time the soldiers came, if they ever did, Slocum and his partner would be long gone.

Or long dead.

"I'll meet you at the other cave. I can find it," Alicia said. She took a deep breath, then said, "I'll wait a couple days, no longer."

"Too dangerous," he said. "Go back to the ghost town where—" He stopped speaking.

"Where the deputy tried to rape me." Alicia nodded slowly, mulling this over. "Staying in these canyons is dangerous. I'll be safer there, and it's a spot we both know." She took a deep breath. "That's where I'll be. But don't look for me at the hotel. Somewhere else. Anywhere else in the town."

Then he saw her change her mind as surely as if he read a book.

"I'll wait here. I need to be with my family as soon as possible. I don't want to be left alone in that horrible town, worrying you'll never rescue them." She crossed her arms and looked fierce. Alicia had made up her mind and brooked no argument.

Slocum had nothing more to say. He pushed past her into the cave and led his horse and the one Loretta had ridden out into the night.

"John, I'm sorry it has to be this way."

He touched the brim of his hat without giving her any other indication he'd heard, then started down the hillside. He heard her crying openly behind him. Slocum felt cornered, and he didn't like it. As he rode, he turned over in his mind what to do if he found Rawhide before he rescued Alicia's parents. Even as he dismounted outside town and hurried toward the mine and mercury separation mill, he hadn't reached any conclusion.

Slocum veered toward the shed where Loretta had hidden when he saw a handful of Mackenzie's gang crowded around the door into the building where he had found Mrs. Watson before. He tried to figure out what caused the sudden interest.

Changing his plan, he left behind that building and went to the gold mine. Linc Watson could be the first one freed. The pair of them could deal better with the woman and her mercury-fogged brain. But as he stepped into the mouth of the mine and reached for a miner's candle, he froze.

From the depths of the mine came a loud argument. At least four men wrangled over their new assignment. Slocum pressed his back against the cold rock wall and sorted out what was being said. Not only had Mackenzie stationed more guards at the amalgam factory, but he had assigned a double shift in the mine.

Slocum edged out and looked around. In a way this made

his next move easier. Find Rawhide Rawlins and get the hell away. Alicia had resorted to extortion to free her parents. He didn't blame her for trying, but he wasn't inclined to appreciate being placed in the position of risking his neck.

He walked toward town, keeping an eye out for roving guards. Slocum quickly realized that Mackenzie lacked the manpower for such blanket patrols. He had taken gunmen from the day shift and assigned them to watch over the miners in the night shift as well as those in the separation plant. Slocum had to make use of the doubling to find Rawlins in town.

Wilson's Creek might have been a ghost town for all the life he found. He realized then how fully Mackenzie kept them under his thumb with threats of the thunderbird. Slocum went to the back of the hotel again and found the window that had given him entry before. He wiggled through and opened the broom closet door to slip into the hotel's lower hallway.

A quick look around the lobby made him smile. Before men had slept willy-nilly on the furniture. Now the lobby was as quiet as a graveyard and as empty of life. He crossed to the stairs and went directly to the room where he had found the stacked books and odd gadgets. Rescuing the Watsons and Rawhide Rawlins seemed less important than finding out how Mackenzie had created the thunderbird. The answer had to be in this room.

He closed the door behind him and lighted a kerosene lamp. Slocum worked up and down the stacks, puzzling over the titles. He saw a book on the table and recognized it as the one Mackenzie had read to Alicia. From the sketches in it, Slocum guessed at Mackenzie's inspiration. An old Italian had designed wings that would fit over a man's arms. Slocum had never heard of such a thing as a bird-man, but Mackenzie was powerful enough to flap and use the makeshift wings to sail through the air.

Rummaging through the rods and pulleys on the table showed Slocum how the wings were built. Leather straps held them to Mackenzie's powerful arms. The bolts of cloth, once a few yards were shaped and stretched taut, made the actual wings. A bird had feathers; Mackenzie used cloth to catch the air. More gadgets left Slocum scratching his head, but one set of claws confirmed all he suspected.

Blood on the curved talons betrayed how Mackenzie had killed. The claws strapped on to his huge, gnarled hands. Then, like a bear, quick, vicious slashes ripped his victim to bloody ribbons.

"You fly down, no tracks, claw your quarry to death, then flap off," Slocum said. It struck him as too complicated when Mackenzie could just shoot his victim. Then he remembered how crazy Mackenzie was. More than this, Mackenzie built fear in his gang and made everyone in Wilson's Creek think he held supernatural powers over the thunderbird.

Slocum whirled about, hand going to his six-gun, when the door opened.

"Wait, don't shoot. You're in danger," Erika whispered. "He's coming back and is sure to find you if you stay."

"I'll get rid of him once and for all," Slocum said.

"He's got a dozen men with him. Please." The red-haired barkeep motioned for him to follow her.

She had gotten him out of a tight spot before. Slocum saw no reason to think she was leading him into a trap now. If Erika had meant him harm, all she had to do was alert Mackenzie to him in this workshop.

He blew out the lamp and trailed behind her. Erika had gone to the rear of the corridor. Voices from the lobby told him not to ignore her warning. Several guards were silenced when Mackenzie roared in anger at them.

Erika turned and motioned for him to forget going downstairs. He ran to join her.

"Inside," she said. "It'll be a tight fit, but we don't dare get caught up here. Going into Mackenzie's room means instant death."

"By thunderbird?"

Erika smiled crookedly.

"He'd like you to think that. You know it's all bamboozling, don't you?"

"I saw the books with plans for wings. Does he actually fly?"

"Come on," she said, prying back a wall board. With an agile twist, she slipped into the tight space beyond. Erika grabbed his coat and pulled insistently. "He doesn't know about this room."

Slocum heard heavy footsteps on the stairs. Whether Mackenzie came up or sent his men didn't matter. Fighting them off wasn't in the cards. Slocum grunted as the rough wooden edges tore at his clothes and skin. Barely had he popped through when Erika shoved the board back into place.

"You can look through here," she told him, pressing close behind. He was aware more of her warm, curvy body than the peephole until she reached around him and tapped the wall beside it.

He bent slightly and positioned his eye to see through the knothole into the hallway. He caught his breath. Mackenzie came down the hall straight for him. For a moment Slocum thought the misshapen man had seen him. Mackenzie flexed his powerful arms, cracked his knuckles, then went back to his room, pausing a moment before going in. The door to the workshop closed with a definitive click that made Slocum sag just a little in relief.

"I saved you," Erika said softly in his ear. "Now it's your turn. I want out of Wilson's Creek."

"You have the run of the place," Slocum said. "You can leave whenever you want."

"It's not that simple. You just watched why not. Mackenzie's got a letch for me. If I tried to get away, he'd come for me pronto. As crazy as he is, he gets something fixed in his head and it doesn't go away easy."

"What do you want me to do?"

"You came back. You got one of the whores away, her and the special one Mackenzie had in the room just outside. Get me out, too." Erika's voice dropped to a barely heard whisper, but he felt her hot breath and then the tiny nip as she worked on his earlobe with her teeth. "I'll make it worthwhile."

Slocum grunted. Her hands worked around his waist, then roved lower. She began kneading his crotch like a lump of dough. And like bread dough, something was rising. Pulling his hips back into her body let her squeeze down even more.

"This is kinda dangerous," Slocum said, even as he responded to her pressing, dancing fingers. "He might hear."

"He might, but I want you to know how serious I am about . . . enlisting your aid." Erika dropped to her knees and turned him around. "I want to seal the deal."

She popped open the buttons on his fly and let his trapped manhood leap out free and proud.

"Oh my, I certainly chose a real champion. You're hung like a stallion."

The rest of her words became mumbled as her lips engulfed his organ. She moved forward an inch and took him more fully into her mouth. Cheeks going hollow with suction, she ran her tongue all over the bulbous tip until Slocum felt as if he would explode. He laced his fingers in her long, coppery hair and pushed her back. She reluctantly followed his guidance. The instant he let up the pressure, she dived back, taking even more of him into her mouth.

The tip of his shaft bounced off her cheek, then she cradled it in her tongue. She made gobbling sounds and moved even closer to take him farther down her throat. The touch of her teeth along with the rippling movement of her tongue almost caused Slocum to get off. He closed his eyes and concentrated on the danger Erika posed. A madman worked on his deadly schemes only a couple yards down the hall. If he heard anything, he would come boiling out.

Mackenzie might use his fake thunderbird talons or call

his henchmen. It had sounded like a small army had joined him in the lobby.

"Umm, you're a tasty one," Erika said. Her tongue made a quick swipe around the very tip of his manhood, then teased the sensitive cleft just beneath the head.

"I have others to get out of town," Slocum said. "I promised them."

"You don't have to promise me—unless you want more of what I offer. The first time I set eyes on you, I knew you were different. You're a gentleman. You're the kind who keeps his word."

Slocum leaned back against the plank, then jerked away, remembering the panel was loose. This rammed him deeper into the woman's mouth. She took him full length, held him erotically, then backed off, panting. She looked up, her emerald eyes glowing in the faint light.

He tried to concentrate on other things. The hidden room was hardly wide enough for him to stand without brushing his shoulders on either wall, but it ran a good fifteen feet back from the false wall. It had to be some kind of building mistake that had been walled over because nobody cared.

"You *will* get me out of here and protect me from him? It's all right if you kill him."

"I'll do that for nothing," Slocum said, remembering the murders he knew Mackenzie had committed.

"I'll help you get the others out. I can pay my way," she said before working down the length of his fleshy spike and teasing the hairy balls dangling below.

Slocum was reaching the breaking point. Erika's mouth knew all the right places to touch, her lips stimulated him wildly, and the occasional snakelike flick of her tongue pushed him to the edge of his endurance.

He stepped forward, forcing her to sit on her haunches, then she continued stretching out in the narrow room until she lay on her back. She lifted her ass off the floor and bunched her skirt around her waist. Even in the dim light

Slocum saw paradise. Dropping his gun belt to get it out of the way, he joined her on the floor. Her knees came up. She grabbed them with her hands and spread herself wantonly.

Slocum inched forward until the tip of his column brushed her soft, moist sex lips. He positioned himself and thrust forward with a smooth, even movement that caused her to cry out. It took all his willpower to stifle his own out-cry. He found himself engulfed by her again, this time a yielding sheath of female flesh. Warmth and wetness surrounded him as he paused, buried balls deep.

"I need you," she said. "Do it, do it," she urged. To empha-size her desire, she tensed her inner muscles and clamped down all around him. It felt as if a hand in a velvet glove milked him. "Now!"

Blood pounded in his ears, and he hardly heard her cries. He drew back, then shoved forward with enough power to lift her off the dusty floor. At first his movement was ragged, then he found the ages-old rhythm of a man loving a woman. But this, too, changed as white-hot tides rose within his loins. His stroking turned ragged again, desperate, and then he lost control entirely.

He spilled his seed as she moaned out her own pleasure. All too soon he began to melt within her hot core.

Slocum sat back and looked at her. Her eyes danced and the smile on her face was positively wicked.

"I could get to like that," she said. "A lot."

"Too bad we had to meet like this," Slocum said.

Erika sat up and moved her skirts around. Legs crossed, she moved close so her face was only inches from his.

"We ought to keep the noise down," she said. "It must be close to daylight and his guards will be going out to their posts."

"He had double the usual crew out at the mine and mercury-gold amalgam plant."

"Why? Something must be wrong."

"He knew I was coming back for the Watsons."

"That their names?"

"And Rawhide Rawlins. You know him?"

"Doesn't ring a bell. Describe him."

Slocum did and finished with, "He's probably paid for a couple months here. He had a passel of money."

Erika looked hard at him, then gave him a knowing smile.

"He owes you, right? But I see all the visitors and nobody like him's come through in the past week or two. Mackenzie might have sent him straight away to the mine. Or the new project, the one north of town. Nobody knows what he's up to but I think he is diverting another stream to add to the water he already takes from Wilson's Creek."

"Might be the water's poisoned when he gets done with it at the mine."

"Heard that's possible," she said.

"So how am I going to get you all free? If I kill Mackenzie, that'd solve the problem. He doesn't look to be the kind who trusts a second-in-command. Cut off the head and the body dies."

"Men have tried. All of them ended up slashed apart by the thunderbird. It only adds to Mackenzie's reputation."

"So how do I get you—and them—out?"

"You promise you won't leave me?" She reached out and stroked over his crotch.

"I won't let you stay here a second longer than necessary," Slocum promised.

"This'll seal the deal," she said, rising and planting a wet kiss on his lips. "Now that we're partners, here's a plan I worked out a while back but couldn't pull off alone."

Slocum listened closely. Erika ought to have been a general. She had worked out the details in a clever, if desperate, escape plan. All they needed was a little luck—and Slocum's Colt.

13

"You get the horses, John. I'll prepare for everything else." Erika held the tin of lucifers Slocum had given her in the palm of her hand, as if weighing them.

"This is only good once," he told her.

The grin she gave told him how much she would enjoy torching Wilson's Creek. She sidled closer and gave him a quick kiss.

"Go on. We don't have much time," she said.

Slocum strode off, heading for the stables Erika had pointed out to him. He took three horses, retrieved his own, and then rode straight for the mine. It was going to be light soon, and the shift would change at the mine. The number of guards couldn't be maintained, and Slocum doubted they would be. Mackenzie had waited for him to free the prisoners. During the day any such attempt would be more obvious. Or so he thought.

Whether he could bluff his way into the mine to free Linc Watson or had to shoot his way in—and out—worried Slocum a mite. He decided to tackle the problem of freeing Mrs. Watson again. With the horses ready, he felt he had a better chance. He rode to the side of the mercury amalgam plant and kicked free of his horse. Barely had his boots touched the ground when he was challenged.

"Who're you?"

Slocum turned and faced a pair of guards positioned just inside the plant door.

"Mackenzie sent me to fetch the accountant woman. He says there's been someone stealing gold dust, and he wants to find out who it is."

Slocum hadn't expected such swift reaction—and realized a split second too late he ought to have come up with a different reason for Mackenzie demanding to see Mrs. Watson. Both guards lifted their rifles to plug him. He was quick, but they had the upper hand. One rifle slug ripped away part of his hat and embedded itself in the wall. The second spanged off his belt buckle, doubling him over.

With a loud *whoosh!* as air rushed from his lungs, he stepped back and sat hard, dazed.

"Finish him off," he heard someone say in the far distance. The ringing in his ears muffled the reply.

But instinct took over. He flopped onto his side, braced the butt of his Colt against the ground, and fired. His shot went low but struck one guard in the knee, sending him hopping about and yelping in pain. Something about the other man's outcry cleared Slocum's head. His next shot ended the man's life, drilling clean through his heart.

The return fire took the second gunman by surprise and slowed him enough for Slocum to use both hands to steady his pistol and aim higher. His slug ripped through the guard's forehead and came out the crown of his hat just as his finger jerked hard on the rifle trigger. That slug went wide but spooked the horses. Slocum rolled and rolled in the filth that had fallen from the air due to vapors from the chemical process inside the building. He sneezed and hurt and forced himself to his feet.

He touched the belt buckle and the silver smear where

the lead had expended itself. The bullet had almost drilled through, but he had been damned lucky. An inch higher and he would have gotten gut shot. An inch lower and he'd have wished for the rest of his life that he had died.

Stumbling forward, he got to the doorway and hunted for other guards. One came from the room where Mrs. Watson tended her columns of numbers.

"What's going on?" the guard called.

Slocum's answer was a shot to the man's chest. Moving faster now, Slocum stepped over the body and into the room. The woman hunched over the ledger and entered her numbers from scraps of paper on the table into the bound book. He wondered how accurate she could be after breathing so much of the mercury vapor that she wasn't in her right mind. Mackenzie probably didn't care, and besides, Mrs. Watson was still a lot more lucid than the Wilson's Creek tyrant.

"We're going," he said.

"I know you. You were here before. But you left."

Slocum saw that the blacksmith who had replaced the rivet he had sprung before had done a poor job. One of the guards might have simply put the cold rivet back through the holes and hammered it flat without heating. The iron rod he had used to pry her free before lay in the corner of the room. Slocum grunted once and the iron shackles fell free.

"We need to get your husband now," he told her. "After that, we're riding to see Alicia."

"I have a daughter named Alicia. Another one named Loretta."

"That's right. You can see them all."

This satisfied Mrs. Watson, and she trailed docilely as Slocum took a quick look around outside the building.

"My, I haven't ridden a horse in I don't know how long. Are the spare horses for Linc and Alicia?"

"For your husband and a friend who's helping us escape. We'll have to ride fast to see Alicia."

"She's such a pigheaded girl. Not like Loretta. Loretta was good in school, but not Alicia."

Slocum left the woman astride the horse talking to herself. He mounted, grabbed the reins for the two riderless horses, and started toward the mouth of the mine. No one had come to find why there had been gunfire. For all he knew, the guards randomly shot their prisoners for sport. But he stood in the stirrups and looked back toward town, waiting for Erika to set fire to the hotel. That would cause enough commotion to get Linc Watson out of the mine and ride along the outskirts of town to pick up Erika.

Slocum recoiled when an explosion rolled over the countryside. A huge pillar of fire rose, followed quickly by oily black smoke. Whatever Erika had done, it had created havoc. Like all towns built slapdash, fire was a constant threat. If the townspeople didn't turn out to extinguish the blaze quickly, every building would burn to the ground. Those made of brick might be left with walls standing, but roofs and doors would be charred and the interiors would be smoldering ruins.

A second explosion told him the hotel was completely destroyed. If the woman had found dynamite, she had used it as part of her arson.

"Get the miners to town. Bucket brigade. Hurry!" Slocum called as guards spilled from the mouth of the mine to see what the ruckus was.

"The hell with that," snarled the guard in the front. "Mackenzie told us never to let 'em out of the mine. Do it, Cole."

"You sure?"

"Do it!"

Slocum went for his six-shooter to stop the guard but saw he had no chance to prevent Cole from lighting a stick of dynamite and tossing it into the mine. The explosion spooked his horse. By the time Slocum brought the gelding under control, dust billowed from the mineshaft. The blast had brought down the roof and plugged the mine. Getting Linc Watson out now would take more time and work than he could afford.

Slocum ignored the cries from the guards as he spurred his horse to a gallop. His plan—Erika's—had gone south fast. It took only minutes to catch up with Mrs. Watson. She rode along fearfully. The noise and confusion from the burning town frightened her.

"Come on. We've got to get my friend before we leave," he told her.

"Where's Linc? Wasn't he supposed to come with me?"

Slocum herded her forward, despite her confusion and demand to know where her husband was. Telling her the truth that Linc Watson had died in a mine explosion wouldn't settle the matter. If anything, it might set her off, and Slocum had Erika to rescue now.

They drew rein directly south of the still blazing hotel. Slocum grew antsy when he didn't see the woman and wondered if he ought to trust Mrs. Watson to stay there while he hunted for Erika. Just as he decided it had to be done, he saw the fiery-haired barkeep running straight for him.

He stood in the stirrups and waved. Erika saw him. And then Slocum saw death flashing down from the sky.

"Duck!"

His warning came too late. A dark figure surged upward above Erika, then swooped down in a powerful dive. In the firelight wicked metal talons flashed. Slocum drew and fired, but the range proved too great for a handgun. He emptied his Colt and wished he had a rifle. He should have taken one back at the mine. He should have—

In a heartbeat it didn't matter.

The birdlike creature swooped low. Erika saw her danger and tried to dodge. With claws raking her and knocking her to the ground, the beast surged upward and away. Slocum heard mocking laughter—a voice he recognized. Somehow,

Mackenzie had strapped on his mechanical wings and soared above Wilson's Creek to dive and bring death to Erika.

Mackenzie banked, rose, and then disappeared into the heavy smoke from the burning hotel. Slocum started to go recover Erika's body, then halted when armed men rushed to pull her to her feet. She sagged, then fought weakly.

She was still alive, but Slocum had no hope of rescuing her before Mackenzie's guards dragged her away, back into town.

"That was the thunderbird," Mrs. Watson said, frightened. "It'll kill everyone Mackenzie commands it to kill."

"That was Mackenzie," he said bitterly. "He's wearing cloth and iron wings."

"Where's Linc? You said you were taking me to Alicia and Loretta."

With a last forlorn look into town, Slocum rode toward the canyon mouth and freedom—for Mrs. Watson.

Slocum got the woman past the guard towers before the armed men arrived—if they would at all. Fighting the fire that Erika had set took precedence over everything else or Wilson's Creek would be reduced to smoking rubble. The stench of burning wood and flesh made Slocum's nose wrinkle as he kept the sight at his back and finally made his way around the bend in the canyon. He and Mrs. Watson were hidden from direct sight, but he still felt uneasiness. More than once he cast looks upward to the canyon rims, expecting Mackenzie to come flying down with his slashing claws.

Knowing the secret of the deadly thunderbird did nothing to ease Slocum's mind. The others believed the spirit bird existed. In a way, it hardly mattered that Mackenzie was responsible for the savage deaths. Dupree was just as dead being killed by a mortal human as he would have been if the thunderbird had been real.

"Up there," Slocum said to the woman. "It's not much of a trail, but it's big enough if you walk the horse."

"Walk? Oh, yes, I am tired of riding. Where is my husband?"

"Alicia is waiting for you," he said to distract her.

"Oh, good." Mrs. Watson giggled like a schoolgirl. She climbed down and began hiking up the steep trail.

Slocum snared the fallen reins, then stepped down from his gelding and followed, tugging to keep the horses from balking. By the time he reached the cave where he and Alicia had spent such a pleasant time, he felt they were safe. Somehow, thoughts of Erika intruded as he looked to the cave. She had dared to help him get Mrs. Watson out of her captivity and probably had lost her life.

"Mama!"

Slocum craned his neck and saw Alicia rush from the cave and throw her arms around her mother, hugging her close. For a moment, Mrs. Watson's mind cleared and she sounded coherent as she spoke with her daughter. Hanging back to allow them time together, Slocum stared back down the trail to the canyon floor. Without consciously realizing it, he looked upward. The daylight bathing the rocks showed sharp edges and deep shadows, but nowhere did he see Mackenzie and his crazy flying gear.

When enough time had passed, Slocum went to the cave entrance and herded the horses inside to stand with Alicia's. The cave had become close, hardly large enough for three people with the horses also stabled inside, but neither of the women complained.

"Thank you, John, for rescuing her. She seems . . . different."

"Mercury can do that. She worked in the amalgam separation plant and breathed in fumes twelve hours a day."

"Will she ever be right in the head again?" Alicia's worry was sincere.

"Sometimes the brain clears up. Might take time and lots of fresh air."

He waited. Alicia looked over her shoulder at her mother,

who sat humming to herself and piling rocks on top of each other, then repeating it when the small tower toppled.

Alicia looked back at him.

"Where's my father?"

"Where's Rawhide Rawlins?"

"I'll tell you when you get my pa back." The set to her chin showed her determination.

Slocum wasn't sure he dared make yet another trip into the town. After Erika's arson, the residents would be prickly and inclined to shoot any stranger on sight. Enough of Mackenzie's henchmen knew him by sight, but so did Mackenzie. He had to believe Mackenzie wasn't completely loco, or if he was, a modicum of cunning remained and knew who had caused so much trouble. Returning to Wilson's Creek would be putting his neck in a noose.

Or letting the thunderbird rip out his guts.

"He's dead," Slocum said. "The mine collapsed as I was getting away with your ma."

"You saw the body?"

"He was in the mine when the guards dynamited the mouth."

"But you didn't see his dead body?"

Slocum shook his head. They had reached an impasse. To go into Wilson's Creek again was suicidal, yet Linc Watson might be alive. So might Rawhide Rawlins.

And Erika.

Damning himself as a fool and maybe as touched in the head as Mackenzie, Slocum backed his horse from the cave onto the trail and headed back for town.

14

Slocum sat astride his horse, studying the guards in the two towers. They showed more attention to their chore than previously. Mackenzie must have put the fear of the thunderbird into them. What Mackenzie thought had happened to his town gave Slocum pause. How he went after Linc Watson, Erika, and Rawlins depended on how loco Mackenzie was.

Finding Watson alive didn't come up with high odds no matter how he played the cards. Slocum considered leaving the man, but he didn't know if he had died in the mine explosion. Digging him out would take more effort than a single man could muster.

Slocum considered that Erika might figure out where Rawhide Rawlins was being held, even if her direct knowledge was limited to places where Rawlins couldn't be. But she had been carried off by Mackenzie's men after being attacked by the thunderbird. Mackenzie wasn't the kind of man to show mercy. If he thought Erika had anything to do with burning down his "nest" and most of his town, her body would be drawing flies by now and the real birds—the buzzards—would be feasting.

Swinging his leg over the saddle horn, he dropped to the ground and found a patch of chalky rock mixed in with the more colorful strata. He licked his finger, rubbed it on the chalk, and then carefully drew a number on his forehead, hoping he hadn't gotten it backward. He had lost track of the date, so only a guess and a prayer guided his finger in the number 10. He wished he had a mirror or a running stream to examine his reflection, but he didn't.

It was a quick ride to the guard towers but felt like an eternity because he saw the rifles trained on him the entire way.

"Hello!" Slocum waved when he came to a spot midway between the towers. "I been out of town." He pushed his hat back to show his forehead. "I need to get back. There's a posse back in the canyons after me."

"When'd you come in before?" The question echoed. Slocum waited until the last faint sound had died before answering.

"A week ago. What's happened? I smell burned wood. You have a fire?"

"You have been gone, ain't you?"

"I said so," Slocum said, putting a touch of irritation into his words. He wanted to seem subservient to Mackenzie's rules, but if he showed himself too servile, bullets might fly in his direction.

"Had a fire last night. You're good to the end of the month. Go on in."

Slocum tried not to show his relief. He had chosen the right month. If he had drawn the numeral 9, his "rent" would have been due.

"The saloon burn down? I got a big thirst."

"Naw, it was away from the hotel."

"I'll stand you a drink when you get off duty," Slocum said. He urged his horse forward.

The hair still stood on the back of his neck as he imagined the rifle muzzles following him, but a quick look over his shoulder told the tale. The guards had already returned to watching the road into town, maybe soon to be filled with a posse.

He wiped his nose on his sleeve as he neared Wilson's Creek. The stench from the burned buildings made his eyes water, too. As he rode slowly toward the tent saloon, he took in the destruction. Erika had done a good job. Not only had she destroyed the hotel and the block of buildings surrounding it, but she had damaged most of the roofs in town. A heaviness settled on him as he dismounted a few doors down from the saloon. Going in there again after he had presented himself as a guard meant he would be found out right away.

Slocum went into a general store and poked around, waiting for the two men talking to the shop owner to finally leave. Even if Slocum had had money, there wasn't anything on the shelves he wanted. Not only was merchandise sparse, but the quality was poor.

"Help you, mister?"

"Just signed up here. Found the saloon just fine but need a restaurant for some grub."

"Ain't gonna do you any good. Whole town's short on rations after the fire. Burned up the supply depot on the far side of the hotel."

"Some drunk fall asleep?" Slocum edged toward what he wanted to find out. The store owner gave it to him on a silver platter.

"Naw, the barkeep over at Mackenzie's done it. Got pissed off at him, I reckon. Nobody's sayin' much 'bout it, but she always was a fiery one." He laughed at his little joke.

"With so much reduced to ashes, she went up with it, I reckon," Slocum said.

"Mackenzie has her in the jailhouse. Not sure what he intends doin' with her. Givin' her over to his gang to have their way was one suggestion, but most folks want him to let the thunderbird take her. Serve her right, destroyin' everything we worked so hard for."

"The thunderbird," Slocum said, almost to himself. Mackenzie kept her alive for some reason, and Slocum thought he knew what it was. Louder, he said, "Staking her out for the 'bird's fitting punishment. When's he going to do that?"

"Never can tell with him. He's so plumb loco, he—" The man clamped his mouth shut and went deathly pale. "Didn't mean that. I meant he's so *mad* that he'll take his time doin' the proper thing. Didn't mean that neither. He's *angry*. That's what I meant. He's angry mad."

"In the jailhouse? Where's that?"

"Down the street two blocks and over three," the man said, his words tumbling out. He wanted nothing more than for Slocum to leave and forget his slip of the tongue. Anyone turning in a citizen critical of Mackenzie could save himself from the thunderbird while watching his victim ripped apart.

"I'll be back in a spell," Slocum said. He gave the shopkeeper a hard look. The man's guilty conscience and abject fear of being called an enemy would ensure he never mentioned that Slocum had ever been in the store.

As thirsty as he was, Slocum avoided the saloon. He could win himself another bottle of whiskey, but that was too risky. His fingers went to his forehead and traced over the numeral there. He'd sweat enough to make the chalk begin to run. From the few men with numbers he had seen, whitewash had given their "rent" dates more permanence. As he walked along the main street, avoiding the still smoking debris piled waist high in places, he wondered where a newcomer forked over his money and received his number. A robbery there would put a considerable wad of money in his pocket, money he could use for bribes and maybe even to buy Linc Watson's freedom.

Even as the idea came to him, he discarded it as too dangerous. Mackenzie kept tight control over the mines and the gold taken from the crushed ore and rock dust. Leaving only one or two of his henchmen to collect such a lucrative toll into the city amounted to an impossibility. More than this, any robbery would be discovered quickly. He had to keep a low profile until he'd rescued all three of the people in town he had come for.

The jailhouse roof had been damaged. Holes had been patched with nailed-down planks. The bars in the back window were sooty except where a prisoner had gripped down and left clean spots. Slocum kicked over a crate and slid it to the high barred window, stepped up, and found himself face to face with Erika.

"You came back," she said, shaking her head. In spite of the soot smudging her cheeks and turning her fingers to black roots, she was still lovely. "What did I do to deserve this?"

"You hid me in the hotel."

Erika laughed. "I hid a bit of you somewhere else while we were both in the hotel. I can't believe a quick tumble made you come to rescue me. You are rescuing me?" The apprehension in her eyes made Slocum laugh.

"I'm not about to leave you for the thunderbird," he said.

"I saw pictures of wings that strapped onto a man's arms. I never believed it was possible to fly around like Mackenzie does, but he has the shoulders and arm muscles to flap all the way to the moon."

"He swooped down on you, more like a bird floating high in the air than using his wings to stay aloft."

"So he glides," she said with a touch of bitterness. "It still landed me here. He knocked me down and clawed me up some so I couldn't get away from his men."

She turned. Slocum saw how her back had been gouged by the iron claws. He held his anger in check. Mackenzie had plenty to answer for. This was only another outrage in a very long list.

"When is he planning on feeding you to the thunderbird?"

She shook her head. "Anytime now. The men need something to boost their morale after having half the town burned around their ears and the mine collapsing."

"They dynamited the mine to keep the slaves from escaping."

"That figures. They are as brutal as Mackenzie is loony."

"You see any trace of a man calling himself Rawhide Rawlins?"

"Keep asking and I'll keep giving the same answer. Can't say I have. Mackenzie has a lot of projects scattered around. North of here he put a couple chain gangs to working on a diversion project to bring drinking water into town since he poisoned Wilson's Creek with tailings and mercury."

As she spoke, Slocum examined the iron bars. The mortar holding them had begun cracking.

"If you have a head start, is there somewhere you can hide?"

"Give me a half hour and I can burrow down in the hills where nobody will ever find me. You want to know where?"

"No," Slocum said.

Her eyes got wide, then she said, "You don't think you're going to get away, do you? If I tell you, you don't want to spill your guts where I am."

"Something like that. I'll be back in a few minutes. Get ready."

"There's a guard in the office," she said. "Mostly he stays drunk. You can go in and—"

Slocum jumped down and walked away while she spun her escape plan. He had other ideas. Something told him that gunning down the jail guard would play into Mackenzie's hands. The only reason to keep Erika alive was to use her as bait.

Slocum had no choice but to grab for it, but he intended doing it on his own terms. With any luck, both he and Erika could get free. With half that luck, she would find her hidey-hole, wait out any pursuit, and escape.

He returned to his horse, mounted, rode slowly down the street until he found a saddled horse, and then unfastened the reins from the iron ring at the corner of the building. He reached over and drew out the rifle from the saddle sheath, tucked it into his empty one, and then walked back to the jailhouse, where Erika still clung to the bars.

The rope fastened on the horse's saddle quickly looped around the bars. Slocum secured the free end to the saddle horn, then set the horse to pulling. It had been trained as a cowboy's pony and understood to keep the rope taut. Only two quick tugs caused the bars to come grinding out of the rotted mortar and bang on the ground.

Slocum dropped the rope and led the horse back to the window. Erika had wasted no time forcing herself through the small opening. She left bits of her dress behind, revealing delightfully bare skin. She left some of that on the mortar frame, too. Then she scrambled about, got her seat, and looked hard at him.

"You come for me."

"I'll track you down," he said. "Count on it." He slapped her horse's rump and sent it rocketing away.

This was the simplest part of the escape. Slocum cocked his head to one side and heard a distant cawing. Mackenzie had been watching the whole time from some high perch still left standing in town. Slocum didn't worry about the man showing himself by flying down, not in broad daylight. That would take away the fear he had built so carefully surrounding the myth of the thunderbird. Whatever he planned would be more direct.

That meant Slocum had to be even more direct.

He rode to the saloon, dismounted, and went inside. Faces turned toward him, but he threw them into instant confusion by yelling, "The thunderbird's killing men in the street! Run! Run for your lives!"

He stepped aside as the customers rushed out—whether to heed his advice or watch others being ripped to shreds hardly mattered. Even the barkeep had fled. Slocum walked behind the bar and began smashing whiskey bottles against the bar and then splashing the fierce booze around. He took a good nip from a bottle that had a label on it. The liquor burned all the way to his belly and gave him the strength to keep going.

When he had sloshed as much around as he could, Slocum drew his six-shooter and fired. The muzzle flame ignited the alcohol on the bar, then spread rapidly. He left, yelling, "Fire!"

The pandemonium increased. Mackenzie had foolishly continued making his bird noises. The best Slocum could tell, Mackenzie was high up in a church steeple overlooking the main street. From there with field glasses, he could watch everything happening in town—and at the jailhouse. The flames from the saloon caught, sending oily black smoke from burning canvas and tarred roofs into the air.

Whatever scouting vantage Mackenzie had in the steeple disappeared. Slocum mounted and rode from town, heading north. He intended to swing around to see what condition the mines had been left in after the dynamite collapsed the shaft. If nothing else, he could rob the mercury-gold amalgam plant of enough gold dust to make his insane rescue trip back to Wilson's Creek profitable. He was still of two minds about Rawhide Rawlins. If the man had taken all the loot from the bank, he was welcome to it if Slocum carted off enough of Mackenzie's gold.

The notion caught in his craw that Rawhide had double-crossed him. He had ridden with the man long enough to get a feel for his real character. Rawlins might steal pennies off a dead man's eyes, but he'd cheerfully give them to a friend in need.

Riding fast, he left behind the town and found himself in country that might have been accommodating with a bit of rainfall. Sere grass all around hinted that grazing a herd would pay off in wetter years. Somewhere in this direction Mackenzie had a crew working to divert another creek, which meant higher in the Badlands enough rain fell or bubbled up from the ground to feed a decent stream.

He found a road and considered following it. He spat some grit from his mouth when he came to the conclusion that satisfying his curiosity about what lay ahead didn't cut it. He had freed Erika. He had to look for Alicia's pa, even if he only reported to her that the man had died in the explosion.

As he turned west off the road, a dark shadow swept past him.

"Son of a bitch!"

Slocum went for his pistol, dragged it out, and turned to look behind when a powerful blow caught him on the side of his head. He got off a shot. Then he tumbled to the ground, stunned. The last thing he saw before he blacked out was a pair of boots covered in feathers crash down hard a few feet away.

15

Slocum groaned and tried to move. For a moment he thought the creaking sound came from his joints. As his eyelids flickered open, he saw that the rawhide strips securing his wrists to wooden poles driven into the ground had made the noise. He strained. His muscles bulged, but the leather strips didn't yield any more and only cut savagely into his flesh.

The fog cloaking his brain blew away when he realized he was stripped to the waist and strung up like a hog in a slaughterhouse. His legs were similarly tied to the poles. Craning his neck, he saw he was in the foothills. The poles had been sunk deeply enough that no amount of jerking about budged them. Tied spread-eagle like this made him vulnerable to any attack. That Mackenzie hadn't killed him outright sent a chill down Slocum's spine.

The smoke he had created setting fire to the saloon to cover his escape had done more than he'd intended. During bright daylight, Mackenzie wouldn't reveal his secret of gliding down to slash and kill in the guise of the thunderbird. But Slocum had hidden his attack with clouds of smoke, and that had done him in.

Futilely jerking at the rawhide only cut deeper into his wrists. Blood oozed from the abrasions. If enough soaked into the leather and it dried, the strips would contract, causing the tension to increase. Slocum doubted his arms and legs would be pulled from their joints, but he already experienced considerable pain. More and he might black out. The only thing in his favor was the sun being lower in the sky. Autumn robbed it of its summer fierceness.

Death from exposure wasn't likely in his future, though. Mackenzie had stretched him between the poles for a reason.

Even as he strained at his bonds, Slocum heard distant cawing.

Mackenzie!

"You crazy son of a bitch!" he shouted. "You're not fooling me. I know you stuck feathers on your body, but you're no thunderbird!"

The cawing sounds turned to mocking laughter. Mackenzie moved about in the rocks somewhere behind and above him. Slocum tensed his right arm and leg, hoping to loosen the post on one side. Only his flesh gave.

He looked up when a shadow rushed past him. Mackenzie banked as wind snapped the cloth stretched on the metal poles strapped to his arms. The powerful shoulders and arms bulged with the effort of holding the fake wings in place. Slocum saw that no amount of flapping would make Mackenzie fly like a bird. All he did was glide and swoop like a buzzard circling on rising hot air.

In spite of himself, Slocum watched the phony bird bank again and then touch down a dozen yards away. Mackenzie jerked and collapsed the ten-foot wings, folding them awkwardly. He lumbered forward. Slocum had seen expressions like this before on men driven crazy. Eyes wide and a touch of drool sneaking from his lips, Mackenzie hopped and bobbed about as if he were a real bird.

"You're not much of a rooster," Slocum said. Goading Mackenzie led in one direction—to his own death—but he

had to change the rules of the deadly game being played
out. Tied up as he was, Slocum could do nothing. Let Mackenzie kill him. But the man might make a mistake and let
Slocum fight back.

"You're going to be a gelding before I'm finished." Mackenzie reached out. Six-inch talons on his left hand looked
rusty with dried blood. "Do you cringe in fear? You will!"

A talon raked down Slocum's bare chest, then worked
lower to prod into his groin. Try as he might not to react,
Slocum moaned as the talon dug deep.

"Does that excite you? Some men find it irresistible."

"You're not a rooster," Slocum said. "You're a capon.
This is what you do rather than screwing a woman—because
you can't perform." It was a pitiful jibe, but Slocum was
getting desperate. White-hot pain stabbed into his chest; a
mere twitch of Mackenzie's other talon would castrate him.

"Oh, I've had women. The one you released. Erika. She
is quite taken by me."

"She never said anything like that when I was—" Slocum
cried in pain as Mackenzie raked his chest and left behind
four deep gashes.

Mackenzie danced about, flapping his arms and sending
the wings to their full extension. He cawed and cackled and
might have been some Indian brave doing a war dance. Slocum watched through eyes tearing from the pain. He caught
his breath as Mackenzie danced closer, then lashed out with
the talons strapped on his right hand.

The iron claws passed close to Slocum's face. One tip
opened a small scratch just under his right eye. The blood
trickled down and left a salty taste in his mouth. He spat at
Mackenzie but missed. The bird-man danced away, pretending he was airborne and circling and diving on fleeing prey.

"Was it only the mercury that drove you loco?" Slocum
called to Mackenzie as he moved out of his field of vision.
"You crazy from that or were you always this way?"

"I dream," came Mackenzie's voice from behind Slocum

and above his head. He had climbed into the rocks to once again take wing. "I read. I'm well educated, you know. I saw the plans for wings and knew that was my destiny."

"You think you really are a thunderbird?"

"Of course I am!"

A talon raked Slocum's scalp as Mackenzie soared from his perch and tried to get lift under his wings. He misjudged and crashed to the ground a few yards in front of Slocum. The only weapon Slocum wielded was ridicule. He laughed at how Mackenzie fumbled about, trying to get to his feet. The wings turned him clumsy.

"Everything you care for will be stripped from you," Mackenzie said after regaining his feet. "Erika? I'll find and kill her." He slashed the air with both sets of talons. "The women you have helped escape from my town? I'll have my way with them and then kill them, too."

"What about Rawhide Rawlins?" Slocum took a shot. Mackenzie showed no recognition.

"I'll gut your horse, I'll—" Mackenzie suddenly stopped his taunting and stood straighter. He cocked his head to one side, dislodging a few of the feathers glued to his scalp.

Slocum watched them flutter to the ground. No wind blew. The only sound Slocum heard was the dripping of his blood onto the rocky ground, but Mackenzie listened intently. Then he raced off, again disappearing from the narrow area Slocum could see.

From the scraping noises, Mackenzie worked his way into the rocks behind Slocum so he could swoop down from on high. But he had given up his torment too quickly.

"What is it, Mackenzie? You running away?"

His words echoed into the distance. Then he heard what Mackenzie already had. Steady hoofbeats approached. Slocum swung his head around to keep the blood from blinding him. The ponies coming directly toward him weren't ridden by cowboys or Mackenzie's gang.

Sioux.

Slocum knew he would receive no more mercy at their hands than at Mackenzie's. Argument would fall on deaf ears. He tensed and tried to pull free again. All he accomplished was cutting off the last of the circulation in his hands. He sagged, then looked up when he heard a commotion among the braves.

Unlike the Sioux party he had found in the maze of canyons, these showed no fear as Mackenzie swooped down at them, screeching like some berserk eagle. Quick, sharp words passed from the war chief to the others. As Mackenzie glided overhead, the chief yanked out a coup stick and swung it at the flying man. The tip of the stick hit a wing, sending Mackenzie spiraling away.

Slocum hoped it would ground him. From the rifles coming to bear, Mackenzie would die from a dozen leaden slugs if he touched down. Somehow, he swirled around and remained aloft. The war chief let out a battle cry and chased after Mackenzie, whacking at him with the coup stick. Mackenzie caught an air current and edged up out of reach, but not out of range. The Sioux opened fire.

Slocum saw part of the cloth on one wing tear away, but Mackenzie wasn't deterred. He banked and dived on an Indian whose courage failed him. He stopped firing and tried to wheel his horse about and flee. Iron talons raked along his back, ripping through a hide vest and sending ribbons of blood sailing through the air.

Mackenzie's arms bulged with the strain of pulling out of the dive. More bullets sought him, but he'd had enough of the fight. Rising on a freshening breeze, the bird-man soared and left the Indian war party far behind.

Slocum saw one Indian vent his anger in Mackenzie's direction, then turn and spot him. The Sioux brave rode closer. Slocum sagged, motionless. The worst that could happen was the Indian leaving him dangling from his bonds. A bullet through his heart would put him out of his agony, but Slocum hoped for more by playing possum.

He smelled the brave's sweat and the horse's lather. Moccasins crunched on the ground yards away. Slocum forced himself not to respond even when the Sioux poked him with his rifle. He couldn't keep himself from bleeding. Dead men didn't bleed, so it would be apparent he still lived if the Indian bothered to notice.

Slocum heard a whistling sound. Eyes closed, he could only imagine the steel-bladed knife coming toward his head, his chest. He winced as the knife tip drew a bloody line along his right forearm and nicked his thumb. The brave said something in Sioux he did not understand, then Slocum was all alone.

Waiting as long as he could, Slocum played dead. When he no longer heard the sounds of horses, he chanced a quick look. The Sioux had taken off.

"Find the son of a bitch and kill him for me," Slocum muttered. He spat blood, choked, then forced himself to raise his head. It proved harder than he'd expected. Blood had dried on his scalp and neck. His face had turned into a bloody mask and any twitch cracked it.

It took him several seconds to realize what had happened when something banged into his nose. The pain working its way down from his shoulder into his right hand brought him out of his daze. The brave had cut the rawhide strap holding his right hand. He had automatically brushed his face, but the hand lacked feeling and he had thought he'd been hit with a meaty club.

Wiggling his fingers brought some circulation back into his hand. The strap around his wrist still cut to the bone but persistence won out. His fingers could grip again. Turning painfully, he grabbed the strip holding his left hand. The force of both left and right hands against the leather caused it to come untied from the post.

Again Slocum's victory proved dangerous. Legs still tied wide apart, he fell straight forward and crashed to the ground. At the last instant he got his arms tucked against his chest and broke the fall. The jolt still made him gasp with new torment rattling through him.

When he had regained some strength, he forced his way back until he could sit and look at how Mackenzie had bound him. Using both hands and kicking hard, he ripped out first one and then the other thong holding him. For several minutes, all he could do was sit and stare. If the one binding hadn't been cut by the Sioux brave, he would have died. Maybe not today but certainly tomorrow.

The Sioux weren't any friends of his, but he owed them for the strange kindness one had done for him.

Getting to shaky feet, Slocum looked around. As far as he could see in front, only rocky terrain and occasional flat stretches reached out to the wall of mountains in the distance. He didn't recognize where he was, but he doubted it was too far from Wilson's Creek. Mackenzie lacked the patience to drag him too far. Besides, wearing the thunderbird wings kept him from too much ordinary activity. Slocum doubted Mackenzie would shed the wing apparatus, bring him to this secret killing place, then don the wings again. More likely he had draped Slocum over his saddle and led the horse here before climbing onto the rocks to get altitude to take flight again.

He walked around the rocks, found a narrow path, and took it to the top of the rocks immediately behind where he had been tied. From the scratches on the rock, Mackenzie had climbed here before launching himself into the air. Slocum looked away from the posts below to a spot some distance behind him.

"You're dead, Mackenzie. You're a dead man now."

He had located his horse, shirt, and six-shooter. After dressing and settling his pistol on his left hip, he felt ready to take on a pack of wildcats.

Or a thunderbird.

16

The closer Slocum rode to Wilson's Creek, the edgier he got. The town might have been a thing alive, a malevolent beast waiting for him to enter and be devoured. The smell from the burned wood had new odors added to it. Some weren't unpleasant. The fire he had set using the whiskey gave a heady tang to the evening breeze, but another odor turned his stomach. During the war he had come across too many fallen soldiers burned to death to ever forget that stench. Whether the citizens of Wilson's Creek burned dead bodies or added to the funeral pyres with live ones gave a speculation Slocum became increasingly reluctant to discover.

He fervently hoped the Sioux war party had tracked Mackenzie and killed him for offending their gods. As cunning as Mackenzie had proven in the past, Slocum had to believe he had returned to the town. If so, the death blowing on the night wind might be laid entirely at his feet.

At his talons.

Slocum touched the ebony handle of his Colt, wanting Mackenzie squarely in the sights. If the Sioux had failed to kill him, Slocum wanted that pleasure.

The road he had found came from the north into town. He headed directly around the edges of what passed for civilization in Wilson's Creek and rode to the mines. Erika hid out somewhere. He wished her nothing but a safe escape. Rawlins, if he was anywhere, might be in the mines or at the mystery project north of town. Linc Watson definitely was in the mine—had been. Slocum had promised Alicia he would rescue her pa, if "rescue" fit what had happened between them. She'd extorted his cooperation with a promise of directing him to Rawhide Rawlins. Not for the first time Slocum wondered if she'd lied to him about even seeing his onetime partner.

He finally decided it didn't matter. Freeing Watson and as many others as he could was worthwhile all by its lonesome. Anything that upset Mackenzie and enraged him made Slocum happier. Rubbing his still sore wrists and aching from the deep cuts on his body every time he moved gave Slocum a constant reminder of Mackenzie and his thunderbird disguise.

The ore-crushing plant worked to reduce the ore to dust. Shackled prisoners turned cranks and moved conveyor belts of the crushed gold ore into the amalgam plant. Huge pillars of steam rose from the boilers where the mercury-gold amalgam was reduced, separating out the gold and returning the mercury to a liquid state to be captured and reused. No matter the destruction in the town, the plant never closed, the ore conveyors never slackened their pace—and that meant the mines were once more disgorging ore.

The dynamited shaft looked the worse for its collapse, but hard work had reopened the tunnel into the side of the mountain. The narrow rails disappeared into the hillside and two empty ore carts had dumped their load at the end, almost ten yards from the mine's mouth.

He dismounted and led his horse to a spot where it wouldn't be seen. Only then did he return and examine the carts. He put one foot on a rail and felt vibration from deep in the mine. Another cart rumbled and rattled its way out with a heavy load of rock.

Waltzing into the mine held no appeal for him. Trying to kill the guards one by one was a fool's errand. From what he suspected about Wilson's Creek, everyone was nervier than a rotted tooth. The slightest hint of anything wrong would bring down the wrath of a small army on his head.

Slocum hiked to the guard shack where he had seen those off duty sleeping earlier. The tiny bunkhouse was empty. He slipped in and lit a lamp to get a better look around. A big key ring hung on a nail near the door. He took it down and examined the half-dozen keys. All looked identical.

He worked one off and tucked it into his coat pocket. As he went to return the key ring, he stopped. On impulse he took a second key and slid it into the top of his boot. Only then did he replace the ring.

He blew out the lamp and returned to where the two ore carts rested at the end of the track. Snatching up a tarp, he crawled into the cart nearest the mine and pulled the cloth over him. Hunkered down in the dark, rough metal cutting at his already lacerated body, he waited.

The vibrations coming up from the wheels grew stronger. He almost cried out when a sudden impact against the side of the ore cart jostled him around.

"Dump that ore. The crusher crew will pick it up. Get all three of the empty carts back into the mine. There's a lot of debris that needs to be moved out right now."

Muffled complaints were met with the sound of a fist hitting flesh.

"You shut that pie hole of yours. The boss wanted double the production this week, and we're behind. Ain't even one shift and we're behind."

A second blow and then Slocum's cart rocked. For a moment he thought it was going to topple off the tracks, but then new grating sounds told him the third cart already retraced its way into the mine. Seconds later, he was tossed about as his ore cart clanked after the other one.

He chanced a quick look out and saw only the intense blackness of the mine's belly. He was being pushed into the mine where he wanted, but a sense of helplessness hit him hard. At any instant a guard might pull back the tarp and find him. Or the shackled miner might see the chance to curry favor with his captors and turn him over. Clutching his pistol, Slocum endured the long trip into the mountainside. When the cart stopped, he had to be ready to act.

The cart stopped sooner than he'd anticipated. He waited a moment, then pushed back the tarp and sat up, his six-shooter swinging about as he sought a target. He was alone. Faint yellow light flickered a few yards back along the tracks. A guard beat at a miner with his fists, then added a kick to the man's midriff as he sank to the floor.

"You don't work, you don't get fed." The guard stalked away, leaving the miner doubled over, clutching his belly.

Before Slocum's finger curled back far enough on the trigger to end the guard's life, he disappeared in the darkness. Getting out of the ore cart proved more difficult than it should have. Slocum ached all over and some of his fresh wounds still oozed blood, plastering his shirt to his body. More than this, the roof was so low he had only a couple feet of room between the cart edge and overhanging rock.

He snaked his way over, lost some skin as he went, then fell hard to the ground. The miner moaned and looked in his direction, then held up a miner's candle to better illuminate Slocum.

"You're not a guard. You got a number on your forehead. I think."

Slocum involuntarily touched the spot where he had written the number. He had forgotten about it until now.

"I'm looking for Linc Watson. Where is he?"

"Watson? Oh, yeah, Watson. I remember the name now. He's working the next drift."

Slocum went to the man and pulled him to his feet.

"You want out of here?"

"You touched in the head? Of course I do!"

"Help me find Watson, and I'll get you out of those irons."

"You do it first."

Slocum understood why the miner had no reason to trust anyone. Considering the man's sad condition, Slocum knew he could keep him from bolting and running.

"We work together and the three of us will be drinking whiskey under the night sky," Slocum promised.

"You have to shoot them off? The chains? Or you got a drift pin? You can pry the shackles off that way. Ain't nobody can pick the lock. Too many have tried."

Slocum fumbled in his pocket and pulled out the key. He shoved it into the keyhole and twisted hard. For a heart-stopping instant, he thought it hadn't opened the lock. Then a dull click signaled the lock giving way.

"You done it. You got me out of the chains."

Slocum was almost bowled over when the man hugged him and began to cry.

"We can't stand here lollygagging," Slocum said. "We don't get out of this hellhole without Watson."

The freed miner pointed back down the tunnel, his hand shaking with emotion. Tears ran down his cheeks. Slocum thought he was going to hug him again.

"I'll hunt for him. You stay here," Slocum ordered. The man nodded and wiped his nose with his dusty sleeve. "Get the ore cart and push it to the branch in the tracks."

"It's not full," the man said.

"It will be when it leaves the mine," Slocum said.

The miner wasn't beyond understanding Slocum's plan. His head bobbed up and down as he went to push the cart. Even empty, the ore cart was almost more than the man could handle. Mackenzie didn't feed his slaves well and treated them worse.

Slocum reached the branch. The one he had been sent

down was virtually empty with all the activity where he had to free Linc Watson. He rubbed his forehead, hoping to obliterate the numeral there. Visitors to Wilson's Creek weren't allowed in the mines. Only slaves and guards. However much of the white number he removed had to do. He pulled his hat low on his forehead and walked boldly down the tracks.

Four miners fitfully used their picks on a vein of quartz. A guard sat on a keg of Giant blasting powder picking his teeth with a long, slender-bladed knife. He didn't even look up as Slocum swept past. And he didn't make a sound as Slocum got a step behind him, whipped out his pistol, and swung it hard. The barrel connected with the back of the guard's head.

Slocum pushed the man to one side and looked around. The miners didn't even notice. Fights between guards might be common or perhaps the workers' wills had been completely sapped and they no longer cared. It didn't matter to Slocum. He used their lethargy to his advantage to go deeper into the mine.

In a small niche hacked out of the rock, he found more blasting powder. The temptation to lay a few feet of black miner's fuse and blow it, completely destroying the mine, passed quickly. Trapping Mackenzie's unwilling miners would be as savage as the guards trying to do the same rather than letting their slaves help put out the fire in town.

Farther into the darkness, Slocum saw a guttering candle.

"Watson?"

The light shifted. The miner turned and looked in his direction.

"You came back," Watson said in amazement. "I didn't think you would."

"After the guards dynamited you inside the mine, I thought you might be dead."

"But you came back for me, even thinking that." The man's pick clattered to the floor as he shuffled toward Slocum. "Alicia must be really persuasive."

"Yeah, she is," Slocum said, not bothering to mention how he had helped Erika escape before coming to the mines. "You see my partner? Name's Rawhide Rawlins."

"Not heard that name. There haven't been new miners for a couple weeks, not that I've seen."

"Come on," Slocum said. "I cold-cocked a guard. If another finds him, all hell's going to be out for lunch."

"There are a half dozen now," Watson said.

Slocum hesitated. He hadn't seen but the one guard.

"Are there other shafts?"

"One branches off to the left. And this one. It's the main source of the ore now."

Slocum stopped beside the powder magazine. He used the butt of his six-gun to smash in the top of one wooden cask, then spilled the blasting powder all around. He picked up the small cask and backed toward where he had slugged the guard.

"You can't blow everything up," protested Watson. "There are innocent men in here, unless you're fixing to save them, too. Are you?"

"No," Slocum said. Then he dropped the almost empty cask, fumbled for a lucifer, and remembered he had given the tin to Erika. Sudden commotion made him look over his shoulder in the direction that would take them to freedom.

"There he is! See? I told you!"

Slocum recognized immediately the voice of the miner he had freed. Whether he had been caught by the guards or had run to them begging for his freedom didn't matter. Four gunmen blocked his way out of the mine.

"You don't want me to light this," Slocum said, thrusting out his six-shooter. The muzzle blast would send out enough sparks and hot lead to ignite the powder.

"The powder. Look at what he's done. A trail of it runs back to the magazine!" Linc Watson cried.

The effect was what Slocum had hoped for. The guards began backing away.

"Keep going," Slocum called. He held up his pistol. He could never win a shoot-out, but he threatened mass death with a single shot.

Three of the guards continued to retreat but one showed some gumption.

"You ain't gonna blow us all up. You'd die along with us." He lifted his rifle and aimed at Slocum.

Slocum had to push the bluff even farther. He cocked his six-gun, made a dramatic move, and shoved the muzzle down as if to apply it to the gunpowder. The last thing in the world he expected was Watson rushing forward, driving a bony shoulder into his gut, and knocking him backward away from the powder trail. Slocum landed hard on the floor, the six-shooter discharging with an ear-shattering roar. He tried to aim it toward the blasting powder for a second shot.

A boot crushed down on his wrist until he dropped the gun. Then the guard kicked the pistol away. In the flickering light from a few miners' candles, Slocum looked up into the muzzle of the rifle held in unwavering hands.

17

"Lock shackles on him," the guard said. Two others rushed over to clamp the irons on Slocum's ankles and snap shut the locks.

"He got a key. He can get free, like he did me," the prisoner said. He cackled when a guard found the key in Slocum's pocket and held it up.

"Yup, that's it," the guard with the rifle trained on Slocum said. "You're a slippery cuss. Now you got to do the work of two men."

"That's because they're letting me go free. I won't be working in the mines no more," said the man who had betrayed Slocum.

"You're right, old man," the guard said. "He has to do the work of two men because we just lost one."

"Lost me, lost me," the man said. Then his eyes went wide and he held out his hands as if he could deflect the bullet that seared into his gut. "Why? Why'd you shoot me?"

"Nobody gets out of the mines, but you done us a favor, so we're doin' you one. You don't have to dig ore now," the guard said. He fired again. This round hit the man in the head. He died on the spot.

"We better get back to work," Watson said.

"The two of you have to peck out twice the ore. If you don't, you stay at work until you do."

As Slocum and Watson shuffled back down the stope, Slocum asked, "Why'd you knock me down?"

"I didn't want to die," Watson said. "You would have killed us all."

"It was a ruse to get the guards to run. The powder burns slow. There'd have been time to kick a gap in the trail."

Watson shook his head, then said, "Sorry. I panicked and thought you were trying to kill everyone."

"Should have," Slocum groused.

"Shut up and get to work. There're the picks." A guard settled down across the small chamber where Slocum and Watson began work on the quartz vein flecked with gold.

Bit by bit, the ore dropped to the floor. Slocum worked steadily but not as hard as he might have. His body ached from all the wounds he had acquired, but he mustered his strength rather than trying to produce the ore for Mackenzie. It might take a spell, but he knew what would happen. And less than an hour after beginning to swing the pick, he saw the guard begin nodding off.

Slocum nudged Watson and said in a low voice, "Keep an eye on him."

"Why? We can't get close to him without rattling our chains. That'd wake him up before we got within five feet of him."

"Might be I can throw my pick and skewer him," Slocum said, enjoying the prospect.

"Men who tried that all ended up dead. There's almost no chance of killing him outright."

"Might be if I had a key to the locks."

"You lost that," Watson said with rising anger. "I never thought Tallman would betray us like that. You set him free?"

"He paid for his stupidity by trusting Mackenzie's men," Slocum said.

"They kept the key."

"Not this one," Slocum said, reaching down into his boot. The shackles restricted his reach but the key finally came free.

A quick look in the guard's direction convinced him he had to act now. The lock opened with a click that sounded like the peal of doom. Slocum froze, worried it would bring the guard out of his stupor. The man stirred, swiped at his nose, then settled back. The rifle rested in the crook of his arm, but Slocum saw his Colt Navy jammed into the guard's belt. That was the weapon he wanted more.

He unlocked the other leg, pulled off the shackles, and gingerly set them on the ground. With careful steps, he went to the guard. He rubbed his hands together to get the dirt off them, then moved like a striking rattler. Slocum grabbed his Colt from the guard's belt; it almost jumped into his hand and felt all firm and secure. The guard snorted and opened his eyes. Then his eyes rolled up in his head as Slocum swung the barrel hard into the man's temple.

"Bring the shackles," Slocum said.

"Kill him. I'll kill him if you don't."

"We're doing this my way. It's better to leave him alive to create a ruckus. The guards will fight and give us more time to get away. If he's dead, they'll come for us right away."

"We can shoot our way out." Watson handed over the shackles and grabbed for the guard's rifle.

Slocum attached the irons to the guard's ankles, then released Watson. He used those shackles to secure the unconscious man's wrists to an ore cart. Only then did he step back. He worried that he was drenched in sweat. It was hot in the mine and he had been exerting himself, but attacking the guard had pushed him to his physical limit. Food, sleep—especially sleep!—would renew him, but not as much as being a free man again.

Without asking Watson to follow, he strode off down the tunnel, slowing only when he neared the larger chamber where Tallman had been cut down. As he expected, the four men listlessly swinging their picks had been left unguarded.

Slocum held up his finger to his lips, cautioning Watson to silence. He pointed to a half-filled mine cart. Rather than argue, Watson slipped past and climbed into the cart.

The nearest prisoner looked up. His eyes narrowed when Slocum held out the key to the man's shackles. Using sign language to indicate what he wanted, Slocum handed over the key before climbing into the ore cart.

The miner started to remove his chains but Slocum whispered, "After we get out. If they see you aren't shackled, they'll know something's wrong."

"How?" the man mouthed.

"Push us out, but be sure they aren't watching when you unlock yourself."

The miner tucked the key into his belt, covered Slocum and Watson with a tarp, then began pushing. The cart creaked and screeched as its wheels finally began turning. The tracks caused the cart to sway from side to side as they yielded, but the motion forward became constant.

"I'll kill them all if I have to," Watson said, clinging to his rifle.

"Better to get away without being seen," Slocum said. "You'll be with your wife and Alicia before dawn."

"Where are they?"

"Safe," Slocum said, then silenced the man. Voices coming from an ore cart would alert even the most slovenly guard.

The cart jostled them and then stopped. A gust of wind lifted the tarp. Slocum grabbed for it and pulled it back down. He looked at Watson and whispered, "We're outside. Wait until we're dumped out."

"The guards will see us. The piles at the end of the tracks are sent to the ore crusher."

"Then we shoot it out, but I think the guards are getting sloppy. They think they've done their jobs for the night." Slocum wouldn't have been too surprised to find the guards passing around a bottle of whiskey to celebrate being so good at their jobs.

He fell silent and gripped his six-shooter when he heard boots crunching on gravel around the tracks. Mumbled orders caused a louder argument. Slocum started to burst up to defend the man who had pushed them from the mine. He owed him more than the key to his shackles for risking his life. He peered out from under the tarp and saw the guard shoving the miner who had pushed them from the mine. The rattle of chains convinced Slocum he had been right demanding that the man wear his shackles. The miner—and they—would be found out if he had rid himself of the chains.

"What's happening?" Watson whispered.

"Quiet," Slocum warned. He couldn't figure out what the argument was about. The miner refused to do something the guard wanted. That much was clear. But what else was there but dumping the ore cart onto the pile at the end of the tracks?

Slocum ducked down when the guard forced the miner back to the cart.

"What's going on?" Watson asked.

"I don't think Mackenzie'd want to waste an entire load of ore," the miner protested.

"Shut up," the guard ordered him. "You're not bein' paid to think. Hell, you're not bein' paid!" The man laughed harshly.

Slocum lost his balance and fell onto Watson as the cart rattled on.

"You want the ore *wasted*?" The miner spoke so loudly that it had to be for Slocum's benefit. What he meant confounded Slocum.

"Do it. Now."

The ore cart slammed hard into a piece of wood nailed

to the tracks to stop it for dumping. Slocum tumbled out from under the tarp before Watson. Instead of sliding onto a low hill of ore, they slid down a steep slope. Clawing at the loose gravel to check his fall, Slocum got a quick look below.

Linc Watson slid past and splashed into a noxious pond of waste from the amalgam plant. He screamed as the thick liquids spewed up into his face. Slocum tried to dig in his toes, to find purchase. He slid faster toward the poisonous pond after Watson.

18

"I'm blind!"

Linc Watson screeched as he splashed about in the waste from the amalgam plant, the slimy fluid drenching him and covering his face. He clawed at his eyes and then choked as more of the water got into his mouth.

Slocum slid down the slope, following the man into the pond. He grabbed futilely until a hard kick drove his toe into the slippery incline and slowed his descent. A kick with his other foot kept him from getting dunked in the pond.

"Quiet," he called to Watson. "They'll kill us if you keep up that commotion."

"My eyes," moaned Watson, but he quieted. An occasional whimper escaped his lips but otherwise he settled down. His feet were in the black water while he sat on the bank, body and head well above the surface.

Slocum edged over, careful to keep from joining the man in the poisonous liquid. When he got behind him, he reached out, grabbed Watson's collar, and yanked hard. He pulled the struggling man from the water so he lay on his back facing the slowly lightening sky. Dawn was their enemy. If

Slocum didn't get them away soon, the guards would spot them.

"Don't rub your eyes," Slocum ordered. "Wipe the sludge away, then blink as hard as you can."

"I can't see."

"You have to or you'll never see your wife and daughter again." Slocum used the only goad he could think of. It worked. "They're holed up in a ghost town on the eastern side of the hills. You go blind and you'll never find your way to them."

"I know the place. We passed that town 'fore we started into the canyons."

Watson dabbed at his eyes and then used his sleeve to get even more swiped off before turning his head to the side and blinking fast and hard. He cried out again, forcing Slocum to reach over and clamp a hand over his mouth. A guard stood above them, outlined against the dawn. Slocum couldn't tell if the outcry had drawn his attention or if something else had stirred up Mackenzie's henchmen.

When Watson stifled himself, still fighting to clear his vision, Slocum reached for his six-gun and steadied it to take out the guard. But the shot wasn't needed. The guard sent a stream of urine arching out until it formed a tiny rivulet that made its way into the pond. Then he buttoned up and left. Slocum let out his pent-up breath and relaxed a mite. That single shot would have meant their deaths when other guards swarmed over to see about the ruckus.

"Everything's blurred, but I can see better. I'm not blind." Watson started to rub his eyes. Slocum stopped him.

"Keep blinking. Don't force more muck into your eyes."

"Feels like I'm bawling with so many tears pouring out." Watson looked up with his bloodshot eyes and smiled wanly. "Thanks. You saved my life and maybe my sight."

"We're not out of trouble yet," Slocum said.

He looked up the slope and saw how slick it was as sunlight glanced off the shiny black surface. Climbing would be a chore, but he saw rocky areas to support their weight. He pointed out the spots to Watson, then started up. After a few of the stones gave way under his weight, Slocum slowed and made certain of every hand- and foothold before pulling himself higher.

Watson slid back a few times but was only a yard behind Slocum when he reached the rim. Slocum flopped onto his belly and grabbed the other man's arm, pulling him to safety.

"I lost the rifle," Watson said.

Slocum thought that was for the best. Watson's anger at being imprisoned and forced to work in the mine, what Mackenzie had done to his wife and daughters—all those reasons increased the likelihood that Watson would fly off the handle in a quest for revenge.

"If we steal horses, they'll know right away."

"The wagon," Watson said. "It's daybreak. If the wagon's leaving, we might sneak out on it."

"What wagon?"

"Every week a wagon's sent south. There's a town on the railroad there. Mackenzie buys supplies using gold dust."

"We might be lucky. With so much destroyed in town, Mackenzie will want to get supplies right away."

"I saw him overseeing a wagon being loaded with the gold dust this morning, right before they sent me to the mine. It always leaves at first light."

"Where's it leave from? The center of town?"

"No, from here."

Slocum got to his feet, helped Watson stand, and turned him around to get his bearings. The man's eyes still watered, but they looked sharp.

"Over there," Watson added, pointing. "The supply warehouse is right there."

Slocum ran to the building, aware that the shift change would bring out double the number of guards. Since Mackenzie had already ordered more of his gang into the mines after the fire, the place would be swarming soon.

He and Watson pressed against the warehouse wall. Slocum opened a door and chanced a quick look inside.

"Four guards. Two are loading the gold, two are already in the driver's box."

"What are we going to do?" Watson talked to empty air.

Slocum reacted fast. He scooped up a rock as he went into the warehouse. He heaved it hard enough to bang into the far wall, drawing all four men's attention. With a savage swing, Slocum decked one guard. The other responded, only to catch a hard punch to his gut, doubling him over. Slocum lifted his knee and caught the man on the chin. From the way his head snapped back, he might have broken his neck. He slumped to the floor and lay still as Slocum hopped into the wagon bed and slid under the tarp.

He reached for his six-shooter when he heard a disturbance behind him but realized Watson had finally joined him.

"The driver and his partner didn't see you drop the guards."

The wagon clanked, creaked, and rattled from the warehouse, drowning out Watson's report. Slocum pulled a canvas bag over and pounded his fist on it. He unlaced the top and saw it was filled with dozens of smaller leather bags.

"This much gold can make a man very rich and very happy," Slocum said.

The wagon hit a rock and sent both him and Watson flying, to crash back down. The sack of gold hardly budged. It would take the wagon to make off with the gold, but Slocum already considered how to get away with the shiny dust. All of it. Mackenzie owed him.

That thought sparked another. Rawhide Rawlins owed him, too. He hadn't located the cowboy, much less found out why he had hightailed it with the bank loot. Getting the Watson family free from their bondage was a start. Rescuing Erika went even farther, but Rawhide presented a different problem.

He drifted off to sleep, exhausted from all he had been through. His body hurt and had passed the limits of endurance. He had no idea how long he had slept but knew when he woke up that Linc Watson was gone.

So was the gold dust.

"Danged wheel's loose," came the loud complaint from up front. "Thought it'd go spinnin' off when you hit that pothole."

"Ain't my fault," grumbled the driver. "You was supposed to tighten the wheel nut 'fore we left, but you was too hungover to do it."

Slocum listened to the pair argue. He was in a dangerous spot. Watson had left with the gold dust. Leaving his rescuer behind was another way of putting distance between him and Mackenzie's men.

Anger built as Slocum turned that notion over in his head. Watson had left him to die after having his wife and girls rescued. Without the key and a helping hand, Watson would have died in the gold mine. He cursed his foolishness telling Watson where they were as a goad to get him to safety. Once he had mentioned Alicia and Mrs. Watson hiding out in the ghost town, Slocum's usefulness disappeared.

"Got a wrench in the back o' the wagon. Gimme a hand with it."

Slocum slipped his gun from his holster, lay flat on his back, and waited. The tarp went flying. The two men jumped back startled when they saw their unexpected cargo.

"Make a move for your six-shooters and you're dead," Slocum said, sitting up.

The wagon's poor condition betrayed him. As his weight shifted, the wagon lurched and the wheel popped off, sending him sliding. The shock of seeing him had worn off. Both men slapped leather. The air filled with lead. Slocum caught a bit of luck when neither of the men proved much of a marksman. He got off a round, sending them scurrying away like frightened rabbits. This gave him the chance to flop over the side of the wagon and land hard on the ground. The tilted bulk of the wagon sheltered him from more slugs sent his way.

Outnumbered and outgunned, he made his way to the nervous team. Working underneath, he unfastened the two horses. He intended to jump on the yoke between them and get away. His luck failed him now. As he stepped up to grab the harness, one horse reared. Slocum was thrown back and landed hard against the wagon.

Momentarily stunned, he failed to hang on to the harness as the horses galloped away.

"The gold's gone. That varmint stole the gold!"

The complaint warned Slocum that at least one man had jumped onto the sloping wagon bed and moved forward. He swung about and flopped on his belly, estimating where the man would be. He squeezed off a couple rounds, shooting through the wagon bed. From the squeal of outrage, he had winged the man.

That still left him in a precarious position. Now he faced two furious gunmen, one of them wounded.

"Give us back the gold, and we'll let you go free," lied the gunman in the wagon bed.

Slocum heard boots scraping across the wood. Moving fast, Slocum rolled from the protection of the wagon as slugs ripped through the spot where he had been. He caught a flash of the man in the wagon bed levering his rifle and firing as fast as he could. It took Mackenzie's man a second to realize Slocum was no longer under the wagon.

Slocum squeezed off a round. He doubted he hit his target, but the rifleman dived for cover. Where the driver had gone didn't matter as long as Slocum could get the hell away. He ran for cover, sliding into a ditch alongside the road as another fusillade ripped through the air above his head.

He checked his pistol. He was low on ammo. If the men firing at him stopped, put into effect a decent attack, and launched at him, he was a goner. He sank down, thinking hard. As his ear pressed into the ground, he heard distant hoofbeats. His luck never improved. That had to be reinforcements sent from the mine to find out what had happened to the men he had left on the warehouse floor. If he failed to get away now, he would end up with shackles on his legs and working the mine again—or worse.

His back and torso ached from the wounds Mackenzie had inflicted with his razor-sharp thunderbird talons. Slocum couldn't rely on the Sioux to free him if he got strung up again.

The vibration from the horses' hooves changed to sound that filled the air. He glanced over his shoulder and saw two distant dark spots coming fast. A quick check of his Colt told him he was in big trouble. Caught between the two in the wagon and the approaching riders, he was a goner.

Sidling along in the ditch moved him away from the wagon. He took a couple shots to keep those men away. If they charged, they had him. He couldn't remember how many shots he had left, but if he had two, it would be a miracle.

"John!"

Hearing his name caused him to perk up and look around. It took a second to realize the two horses galloping toward him carried only one rider—Erika. The horse with the empty saddle was his gelding. He tried waving but drew fire and fell back. She would make a target of herself if she came closer to rescue him, but he would get himself filled with lead if he stood and ran to her.

She understood the problem, aimed his horse in his direction, and gave its rump a hefty slap. She stayed out of range as the gelding thundered toward him. When he saw the horse's path, he acted. Gathering his legs under him, he sprang out, dodged, and wove about crazily as the driver and guard fired wildly. His horse raced past. One chance. That was all he had. His fingers snaring the reins, he took three quick steps and jumped. His fingers curled around the saddle horn and then he was being dragged along until he kicked hard and became airborne. He landed in the saddle and immediately shifted his weight to steer the horse away from the road.

From behind he heard angry cries and finally the bullets stopped seeking his flesh. He had ridden out of range. The gelding strained on until Erika came alongside.

"You can ease up now," she called.

He complied and let the gelding slow until it came to a halt.

"You're a sight for sore eyes," he told her.

"I happened to be out for a morning ride and thought it'd be good if you joined me."

"Right about now, there's nothing I'd like better."

"You stirred up everyone in town 'bout as good as I did. It took the better part of an hour for them to put out the fire. Mackenzie has been ranting and raving. Offered a hundred-dollar reward for you."

"That's all?" Slocum said dryly.

"I think you're worth more. You came back for me."

"Watson lit out with a bag of gold dust. Mackenzie's not going to like that when he hears."

"Any idea where he's going? Seems we ought to be cut in, considering he would still be swinging a pick in the mine if not for us."

"I told him his wife and daughter were going to an abandoned town on the other side of those hills." He pointed to the red-and-yellow stratified mountains due east. "I like the idea that he settle up since . . ." Slocum's words trailed off.

Rawhide Rawlins had money that was his. A share of it, at least. They had earned that money, and thinking of it as stolen from the bank hardly counted. It was money owed him, Rawlins, and Dupree by a scoundrel of a rancher. But a share of Mackenzie's dust would make a fine replacement.

"Can we find him?"

"He was on foot," Slocum said, "but I don't know how much of a head start he has." Carrying the heavy sack of gold dust would slow any man. "I don't cotton much to taking the road through the hills since we'd have to pass those damned guard towers."

"We're miles south of that canyon," Erika said. "I saw a map of the entire area Mackenzie uses. He's got his projects up north and built this road south to Upton."

"That's where he swaps the gold for supplies?"

"A train that comes through every week or so. We might catch it," she said hopefully.

"I don't have two nickels to rub together."

"Me neither," she said, scowling. "You say Watson is on foot? And you know where he's headed?"

Slocum smiled. He liked the way Erika thought.

19

Two days later Slocum still hadn't found Watson's trail, but he and Erika had made good progress finding their own way through the winding canyons of this stretch of Badlands. The colorful rock turned vivid reds and yellows in the sunsets and sunrises, making the ride pleasant.

Riding with Erika made it doubly so. They had finally reached the point of exhaustion and stopped for the night. Slocum stretched and fumbled to pull his blanket up over his shoulder. It had been a chilly night and the morning carried an icy stab to it that promised winter approaching fast. He groped for the blanket but failed to find it.

What his fingers did touch caused him to roll over. A broad smile came to his lips. Erika had stolen his blanket and had pulled it around her naked shoulders. The dawn light turned her breasts alabaster even as the cold turned her nipples into taut little pink buttons. He had reached out for the blanket and found the thatch between her legs.

"That wasn't an accident, was it?" he asked.

"Took me a while to position myself so you'd touch me

there if you hunted for the blanket," she said. She clamped her thighs together and trapped his hand.

He moved it up across satiny skin and found the moist spot at the juncture.

"I'm ready for you, John. Been ready for a long time. I wondered if you were going to sleep away the entire day."

"Got a good reason now to get up."

She reached out and pressed her palm into his crotch.

"Yeah, you have." She squeezed down, then moved to pop the buttons on his fly and release the pillar of lust she had built.

The instant it emerged into the cool morning air, she dived down on it, engulfing it with her mouth. She sucked and licked and caused him to arch his back. He wanted to slam himself upward as hard as he could, but her fingers toying with his balls and her tongue stroking along the underside of his manhood controlled him fully. She began bobbing up and down, keeping a powerful suction applied to his length.

Slocum sank back to the floor of the cave where they'd spent the night. The first night had been frantic for them, sure that Mackenzie's men were on their trail. He had spotted spoor from several riders who had passed only a few hours earlier. Pushing their horses to the limit, they had been physically spent.

That had been followed by another day of wandering through the canyons, worrying that they were going to be seen or get so lost they would die in the rocky wasteland. But the previous night had brought some relief. Slocum recognized terrain farther along the canyon and knew by midday they would reach the ghost town where he had sent the Watsons.

Knowing the destination let them both relax. And enjoy the scenery some more.

Slocum ran his hands over Erika's back, pulling the blanket up over her bare ass. He cupped those curvy buttocks and squeezed down every time she sank another inch down his shaft. When he worked his way around a bit farther, he stroked over her moist nether lips and finally ran a finger into her hot interior. Her gasp at the intrusion gave them both a surge of desire.

Slocum fought to keep from spewing forth as her lips worked on the sides of his column and her tongue wiggled against the sensitive underside. Then she let him pop out and licked her lips. She looked him squarely in the eye.

Words weren't necessary. He gripped her firm rear and pulled her around so she straddled his waist, legs spread and her crotch directly over the tip that had been in her mouth.

"Ride 'em, cowgirl," he said as she lowered herself and took him fully within her clutching tunnel.

"Oh, yeah," she said softly. Closing her eyes, she began rising off the throbbing rod within her. When only the plum tip remained within her, she paused, then lowered herself again to take him completely.

Slocum reached up and cupped her breasts. The warm white globes flowed pliantly under his grip. He caught at the cold-hardened nipples and tweaked. The blood pulsing into them made the points even harder. From them he stroked down into the valley between her tits, circled around them, and slowly moved back up her body to stroke her cheek.

She turned her head, caught his finger in her lips, and gave it the same treatment she had performed lower on his body. All the while her restless hips moved up, down, in a slow rotary motion that stirred him about within her like a spoon in a bowl.

He felt sweat beginning to bead on her cheeks and body as her arousal grew. Her hips flew like a shuttlecock now, creating a friction between them that threatened to burn Slocum to a nub. He wanted more and told her.

Erika's body went berserk with desire. She ground her crotch down into his, tightened her strong inner muscles, and only then did she rise slowly. Once at the apex, she slammed back in with a wet sucking sound that caused them both to gasp in reaction. A few times moving up and down like this finally robbed her of her control. She began a movement so strong and quick that neither of them could hold back any longer.

Slocum felt the burning hot sensation deep in his balls. As the woman moved all around him, the heat rose. He fought to keep from spending himself. He wanted this to last forever. But her body was too insistent and her movements too fast for that. He jetted out his load into her as she let out her own loud animal howl of release.

They continued to grind together for another few seconds and then she sank down, her breasts pressing into Slocum's chest. She twisted about and finally straightened her legs so she lay completely atop him. Her weight pressing along the entire length of his body caused vague stirrings again, but he was too tuckered out to have it amount to anything. For the moment.

"I think I'll rescue you again," he said.

"And I'll have to save your worthless hide, too," she shot back.

"Worthless? You didn't think so a second ago."

"That was then," Erika said. "Now? Nothing but a limp worm." She reached down between them and grabbed at his once tumescent organ and gave it a squeeze. "Oh my, there's something going on again. I have misjudged you, John."

She began stroking up and down but only tiny twinges rewarded her effort. He had been through too much to respond again this quickly.

"Later," she whispered.

"Count on it," Slocum said.

"Oh, I will." Erika snuggled down, then said, "Do we have to go after Watson and the gold?"

"It's not just the gold," Slocum said. "Alicia Watson claimed to know where my friend is."

"Rawlins," she said in a tired voice. "I'm beginning to think you like him more than you do me."

Slocum was loath to tell Erika more. Rawhide had been a friend as they rode the range, but it rankled how he had stolen the loot from the bank robbery. He wanted to have it out with the man if he had reached Wilson's Creek. From everything Slocum had seen where the firefight had been in the canyon, Rawlins had gone with Mackenzie's gang to the town. Answers to important questions lay there—or could be answered by Alicia.

"You can stay here while I go after the Watsons."

"Not if it means you're going to get back Mackenzie's gold dust. I heard how much got sent to Overton. It can keep us both in luxury for quite a while." She pushed herself up so she could look down at him. "That is, if you're planning on sharing."

"I owe you more than a roll in the hay," he said. "Whatever I get back, half is yours."

"Deal," Erika said. "I've been used and abused by Mackenzie and a dozen men before him. You're not like them, John Slocum. And if you are, I swear I'll track you down to the ends of the earth and cut off, oh, I don't know." She squeezed down hard on his crotch. "But I'm sure I'll think of something."

"Still got a use for them."

"If that usage includes me, we have a deal."

He kissed her to seal the promise, then eased her off so he could get dressed. The dawn had changed to midmorning now, but he wasn't in much of a hurry. The ghost town where he had directed Alicia and her mother lay only a short ride away.

"We just ride up and you ask your questions at the point of a six-gun?" Erika asked.

"Something like that," he answered. He had put himself into danger enough by sneaking around. The direct approach worked best, and he intended to find what he needed from Alicia—and ask about the gold dust Linc Watson had carried off.

That bothered him. The man hadn't been in the best of shape working in the mine. After dunking in the pond of noxious sludge, he had ended up almost blind and debilitated. Still, a man's lust for gold produced powerful results.

After he and Erika emerged from the tangle of canyons, and had ridden a ways into the afternoon, Slocum drew rein and pointed to the tight knot of ramshackle buildings.

"There's the ghost town."

"Hard to call it a ghost town with that many people in it," she said.

Slocum squinted in the bright sun and finally saw what she already had. Five horses were tethered near a trough. The gleam of light off the water in the trough showed someone had fetched water for the thirsty horses.

"They're saddled. Those aren't Sioux ponies," he said.

"Mackenzie's men?"

Slocum hated to admit it, but Erika's guess fit all the questions.

"I'll sneak on into town when the sun sets and—"

"That's a lawman," she said unexpectedly. "See the badge?"

Slocum shielded his eyes a bit more and saw the man who had drawn her attention. His stomach knotted. He recognized the man's uneven gait.

"That's Marshal Hillstrom from the next town over. Halliday."

"You don't sound like you're on speaking terms with him."

"There was a little disturbance in Halliday."

"With you and Rawhide Rawlins?"

"And another cowboy name of Lee Dupree."

"So this lawman's as likely to fill you full of holes as Mackenzie?"

"Don't know if he'd shoot first and think about arresting me later, but I'm not taking the chance." Slocum rubbed his stubbled chin as he thought. "You head back toward the mountains and find a place to camp. I'll join you when I can."

"Why don't I backtrack the way we just rode? That'll avoid Wilson's Creek and take me toward Overton. Catching the train there looks to be a good idea if this part of the Dakotas is overrun with lawmen wanting your hide, not to mention Mackenzie and his gang."

She hastily leaned over and gave him a kiss, looked at him strangely, then wheeled about and headed along their back trail. Slocum glanced over his shoulder and saw she had done the same. He watched as she dropped down into a ravine and disappeared from sight. Considering what lay ahead of him, this might be the last time he ever saw her.

He dismounted and walked his horse closer to the deserted town, biding his time until sunset. Instead of thinking about all he had to find out and overcome, Slocum's thoughts turned more to Erika. Even if he failed to find any of the gold dust or loot from the Halliday bank, sharing a trail—and a bedroll—with her wouldn't be a bad thing. Nothing about her had warned him she sought only money.

When the sun dipped low behind the mountains, turning them into blazing ochre and subdued browns, he went straight for the old general store where the horses were tethered. They nickered as he approached, giving him a chance to see what response that caused. A deputy came from inside, a rifle in the crook of his arm. He gentled the horses but paid no attention to what might have upset them.

Slocum worked his way to the rear of the store. Wall planks had rotted out, making it dangerous for him to move. He had to be certain no one inside happened to be looking in his direction as he passed from one solid area in the wall to another.

Alicia's voice caused him to squat down and peer through a knothole. He recoiled when he heard the marshal's voice, too. They were talking in low tones, and from what he could tell, they said things that would upset Alicia's ma and maybe send her pa out hunting for a shotgun. He saw hardly more than dark outlines moving, shadows cast on the far wall by a kerosene lamp set on the floor near the door. This was a back room for the general store, but it had been stripped bare, leaving only broken shelves and litter on the floor.

"There's a house on the edge of Halliday where you can be real comfortable," Hillstrom said.

"How far is it from your house?"

"Next door, my little darling. We can see each other all night long and nobody's close enough to know or care."

"My parents would object."

"There's a nice place for them on the other side of town. With your ma the way she is, Linc's not going to head back East like he's been wanting to do."

"Let them go, Hill," Alicia said in a voice laden with longing and not a small bit of lust. "I'm old enough to be on my own—with you."

Slocum edged around and saw them kissing. He had to find out if Alicia had lied to him about seeing Rawhide back in Mackenzie's hideout. If this went much farther, he might have to wait all night long. Then luck came to his side of the table again.

Alicia hastily pushed the marshal away and whispered, "My pa! That's him thrashing about. He's awake."

"After all he's been through, it'll take a couple weeks to get his strength back." The marshal kissed her again. Alicia was willing, but the sounds from the main room in the store caused them to break off again.

"You see to him. I'll wait here. For you," Alicia said coyly. She unbuttoned her blouse halfway down to reveal those perfect breasts Slocum remembered from the time they'd spent back in the cave.

"I'll make it fast."

"No need to hurry. I don't like it when a man hurries," she said.

"I'll be sure he and your ma are both sound asleep."

The marshal ducked out of the room, giving Slocum his chance—his only chance. He ran his fingers around the board and yanked hard. The creaking and snapping as nails tore out of the rotting wood came louder than he had hoped. Tossing aside the board, he squeezed through into the back room.

Alicia reacted to his sudden appearance. She pressed against the far wall, then started for the door to get help from the marshal.

"Don't move," Slocum said in a low voice that carried a steely edge.

"John?"

He moved closer. The dim light cast by the guttering lamp testified to how badly its wick needed trimming. He picked up the lamp and held it out so he saw her better. That worked for her to see him, too.

"I thought you were dead. Pa said you were in the wagon going to some town, but you'd died."

"If the marshal comes back, I'll have to shoot him."

"Hill? No, you can't do that. I—"

"I heard," Slocum said. "Tell me what I want to know and you won't see me again." He silently added that he hoped he would never see the marshal again either.

"About your friend?"

"Rawhide Rawlins. Were you lying so I'd get your family out of Wilson's Creek?"

"No, I wasn't. I saw a man like you described right after I got caught. They moved me around, but I saw him and half a dozen others being loaded into a wagon."

"Going south?"

"No, north. I don't know why. You . . . you rescued me a bit after that."

"Rawhide was all chained up?"

Alicia's head bobbed up and down. She cast a quick look toward the door. On the other side Marshal Hillstrom talked quietly to Linc Watson about his wife.

"What's the marshal think of your pa showing up with so much gold?"

"What?" Alicia took a step toward him. "I don't know what you mean. Papa said you were dead. He was bounced out of a wagon. He walked for hours until he found a horse all saddled up. There was blood on it and a Sioux arrow stuck in the leather."

Concealing so much gold dust made sense if Watson didn't want to turn it over to the marshal as being stolen. Explaining how he had come by a hundred pounds would be difficult. That set Slocum thinking in different directions. Watson's legs barely supported him, and he was damned near blind. Lugging so much gold would be difficult for a fit man. He might have hidden it, though.

"What did your pa say when the marshal and his posse found you here?"

"He was relieved. All he wants to do is go back East with Ma."

Truth rang in Alicia's words, but that didn't mean her pa hadn't hidden the gold somewhere, intending to recover it later. Marshal Hillstrom showing up changed everything, if Watson had the gold.

"Please believe me, John." She looked distraught, shifting her eyes from him to the door, as she expected the marshal to return any instant. "That's all I know about your friend."

Slocum put the lamp down on the floor and stepped back. He squeezed through the broken board as Hillstrom returned.

"Your pa's in worse shape than I thought, Alicia," the marshal said. "He can hardly lift his arms. If he hadn't tied himself to the saddle the way he did, his body'd be along the trail out in the hills."

Slocum slipped away and went to find the horses. The posse had left them unguarded, but it wasn't the horse Slocum wanted. It was the gear. He found a saddle with an arrow still stuck in the pommel, ran his hand all over it. He examined the skirt and cantle closely, put his nose almost against the leather. Only when he felt sure no gold dust had leaked out—or anything heavy had been strapped to the back of the saddle—did he go back to his own horse.

Linc Watson might be lying to his daughter and to the Halliday marshal, but Slocum didn't think so. He hadn't ridden with the heavy sack of gold dust. There wasn't any trace to be found.

He reloaded his six-shooter with the few rounds he had left. He had to avoid a protracted gunfight because he would surely die with only four rounds riding in the cylinder—all the ammo he had.

As Slocum rode straight into the canyons leading to Wilson's Creek, he mulled over everything he had been told and had seen with his own eyes. If Watson hadn't carried the gold back from the road to Overton, it was still out there somewhere.

And Rawhide Rawlins was working on Mackenzie's water diversion to the north of Wilson's Creek.

20

He had followed this trail often enough that he knew where to ride to keep out of sight, where the high spots were that Mackenzie might perform his deadly leaps wearing his thunderbird wings and, most important, the places the gang hid to trap anyone foolish enough to ride into Wilson's Creek. But this time Slocum kept an eye out for something more.

The spot where he, Alicia, and Rawhide had camped passed soon enough, but if she was right that Rawhide had been captured, he would have bought his way out using the bank money. While the gang might have stolen it, Slocum doubted they would try to double-cross their boss. Mackenzie held them all in slavery as surely as if they had chains on their legs by threatening them with the thunderbird's vengeance. If Rawhide hadn't bought his way into Wilson's Creek, he had hidden the loot somewhere along the trail.

Eliminating the spots too difficult to reach if he were being attacked, Rawhide had only a handful of suitable places open to him. As Slocum rode the trail, he saw rocks piled atop one another in a curious fashion. No amount of weathering or a random avalanche created such a hill. He dismounted and kicked at the rocks. They tumbled over, revealing a burlap bag. A quick tug unearthed it.

"I'll be damned," he said softly. A quick glance in the sack assured him the money was all there.

Rawhide Rawlins had hidden the money rather than let it fall into the hands of outlaws. He had paid for that devotion with his freedom and maybe his life. Once he had entered Wilson's Creek and heard the rules, Rawhide could have offered up the money as his "rent" but he hadn't. The burlap bag Slocum held was mute testimony to that.

Slocum swung the bag over the rear of his saddle, mounted, and rode for the guard towers. He watched for a looming presence along either canyon rim, but Mackenzie never put in an appearance. As night fell, the towers turned darkly menacing on either side of the road. The other guard posts had already been abandoned, telling Slocum that Mackenzie still ruled the town with an iron talon.

As much as he wanted to put a bullet through the fake thunderbird's heart, Slocum skirted the town. His horse shied repeatedly at the burned smells drifting on the night breeze. Mingled with the burned wood came the scent of roasted flesh. Rather than burying the two fires' victims in a mass grave, Mackenzie burned their bodies. It had to be done for sanitary reasons, but Slocum felt his belly twisting into knots as he rode a little faster to put it behind him.

Before, he had headed for the mines. Now, he pointed his horse's face to the north, where the water project sought to bring fresh water to town.

When he left Wilson's Creek far enough behind to appreciate the clean, cold air, he felt better about rescuing Rawhide. A quick glance behind at the bag of money told him he had to set the man free. Glad that his initial belief was correct— that Rawhide would never cross him, not after all the time they'd spent working together and on the cattle drive, watching each other's backs and developing a real friendship—he concocted what ought to be a simple rescue plan.

Slocum had few enough friends. Knowing that Rawhide had not betrayed him or taken the money for his own gave him a certain amount of satisfaction.

He heard the sound of water gurgling before he saw the streambed. This creek flowed sluggishly, hardly wider than he could step across. He followed the ripples in the water farther north toward the foothills until he saw what Mackenzie had planned. A dam held back the flow.

It took a few minutes to get the lay of the camp. A dozen men slept at the base of the dam while two tents pitched farther away glowed with lamplight. The tents held the guards. Their slaves slept under the stars.

Slocum made sure the guards were intent on their card game in one tent and snoring loudly in the other before going to the dam. The water penned up behind the carefully positioned rocks and earthen filling would be released when the workers dug a deeper diversion channel to town.

Only after he had located the equipment being used for the construction and taken a hammer and chisel did he go to where the prisoners slept. They had threadbare blankets pulled up around their shoulders. Some, skeleton thin, shivered although the night wasn't that cold yet. Slocum saw that they suffered from a variety of diseases. Mackenzie might send the men with ague and other ailments here rather than have them infect his gold miners. The fresh air might heal the sick men, though Slocum suspected Mackenzie feared an epidemic spreading in the confines of his gold mine and wiping out all his most productive workers.

So why had Rawhide been sent here? Slocum had the cold feeling he was again wrong about finding his friend.

Carefully stepping over the sleeping men and pulling back the blankets covering their faces, Slocum finally found Rawhide Rawlins. The man looked the worse for wear. His face was a welter of half-healed cuts and in one place a new scar already angled from the middle of his forehead, over his eye to his cheek. The size and placement hinted at a pickaxe used on his head.

He put his hand over Rawhide's mouth to keep him from crying out as he shook the man awake. Eyelids flickered and finally opened. His eyes had clouded over, and Slocum wondered if he saw anything beyond the end of his nose. But his hand on Slocum's was strong and shoved it away.

"Havin' trouble breathin'. Don't cut off my air, Slocum." He sat up, rubbed his nose, and then closed one eye to get a better look. "Never expected to see you again. Heard tell you was et by the thunderbird."

"He couldn't stomach me," Slocum said. "Get your shackles where I can see them." He hoisted the hammer and chisel. "Cover the iron with your blanket. Don't want to make too much noise."

Rawhide did as he was told. His hand shook. Slocum wondered if it came from excitement at being released or if some more tenacious malady clung to him that explained why Mackenzie had sent him here rather than using him in the mine.

A quick placement of the chisel followed by a sharp rap popped open the shackles.

"Best I felt in a week," Rawhide said. He looked around at the other fitfully sleeping prisoners. "What are you gonna do 'bout them?"

"If I cut off the chains, can they run?"

"Most all can. Will," Rawhide said. "Those what can't, the others will help. But they got the guns. We don't." He lifted his chin and pointed Indian style toward the two tents filled with Mackenzie's gang.

"You know how to plant dynamite?"

"Been doin' that to blast rock for that damned dam."

"Fetch the sticks you need, along with blasting caps and five minutes' worth of miner's fuse. That dam ought to be returned to pebbles."

"Good as done, Slocum, good as done." Rawhide got to

his feet and teetered away, his legs barely working. He forced himself to take strides longer and more natural now that the chains had been cut off, but his progress was slower than Slocum had hoped.

He awakened the other eight men in turn, whispering what he expected of them, then removed the chains. The clank and snap of iron sounded like thunder with every stroke, no matter how he muffled the blow, but the guards paid no heed. When Slocum had all eight men together in a huddle, he spoke quickly and low.

"You light out. Don't much matter which way you go. But I ought to warn you that Wilson's Creek is half burned down and the gunmen left there are willing to shoot anyone they see."

"We kin go on north. There's a whole mess o' canyons where we kin get ourselves lost," volunteered a smallish man. "The army post is that way, too. Might be a patrol finds us 'fore we starve to death or die of exposure."

"Get the cavalry down here to bust things wide open," Slocum said. He remembered how Alicia had intended to report Mackenzie to the army. He doubted her resolve had lasted now that she and the marshal were getting on so well. "Me and Rawlins will make sure the guards don't come after you."

"Gimme a knife," said another. "I'll cut their throats while they sleep."

"All of you, go," Slocum said forcefully. "You stay and you're likely to get killed."

Two of the men wanted to fight. The remaining six convinced them Slocum's plan had more merit. Between them, three being supported by others, they began the long hike to the cavalry post. Slocum doubted many would make it, not in their condition, but dying free was a whale of a lot better than being worked to death in shackles.

Slocum retrieved his horse and rode around to the rope corral fashioned between three trees. He saddled Rawhide's horse, then chose two others before cutting the rope and releasing the remainder. By switching off to the spare horses as they rode, Slocum hoped during the next day to put sixty miles or better between him and this goddamned prison Mackenzie had fashioned.

When the horses galloped away, the guards finally twigged to something wrong in their camp. Slocum galloped off with the three horses trailing him as the guards opened fire. The confusion spread when they discovered all their prisoners had disappeared. He rode straight for the rocky dam where Rawhide sat on a rock, looking forlorn.

"What's wrong?" Slocum called. "We got the whole camp coming down on our necks."

"I ain't got a match. No way to light the fuse."

Slocum fumbled in his pocket, then remembered all over again how he had given his matches to Erika for her arson. He glanced back and saw the guards running hard toward him since astride his horse he was the most visible thing in the camp.

"Get on your horse," Slocum said. He waited for Rawhide to mount painfully, then whipped out his Colt, aimed, and fired straight into the blasting cap crimped down on a stick of dynamite.

The explosion staggered his horse, then set it running like its tail was on fire. Rawhide galloped right behind, bent low. His moans of pain sounded above the hammering hooves and the rifle fire from behind them.

Then a creaking sound like a huge giant rusty hinge opening filled the air. The dynamite had weakened the base of the dam. The water pressure behind finally won over the rock and burst out.

"That ought to drown the lot of 'em like rats," chortled Rawhide.

Slocum slowed his headlong pace, and Rawhide did the same. Slocum passed over the reins to one of the spare horses.

"Switch off between your horses and you can put a lot of miles behind you."

"You ain't comin' with me?"

"I've got business to attend to way south."

"Slocum, it's been a pleasure. Don't rightly know how I can thank you fer gettin' me out of that jam." He thrust out his hand and shook with more strength than Slocum expected. "Best I kin do is tell you where I hid the money from the Halliday bank. You know that spot—"

He stopped in midsentence as Slocum reached behind him and swung the burlap bag around. He handed it to Rawlins.

"You found it!"

"Keep it. All of it. You're about the best partner I ever had on the trail," Slocum said.

"But you're deservin' of it. Half, I reckon, since Lee got himself kilt and all."

"Don't flash it around, and don't go back to Halliday. The marshal's looking to make himself out a hero to a new sweetheart."

"How do you know all this, Slocum? I swear, you keep yer ear to the ground better 'n anybody I ever did see."

"The men back at the construction camp might be dead or they might be squealing for a posse of Mackenzie's henchmen from town. Get out of here right now and you'll be just fine."

"Watch your back, Slocum." Rawhide Rawlins gave him a sloppy salute, then wheeled about and galloped away, the bag of money flopping in front of him where he'd secured it to the saddle horn.

Slocum waited for him to disappear into the night, then got his bearings from the Big Dipper and knew he had to ride fast because of a storm brewing. Clouds obscured half the sky and the distant mountains were backlit by lightning.

A heavy rain might be just what he needed to cover his tracks as he headed toward the road to Overton. If Linc Watson hadn't been telling a tall one, a hundred pounds of gold dust waited for him somewhere along the side of the road.

21

The storm moved closer but never dropped the rain promised by the gusty wind. Slocum rode through the night and just at dawn found the road to Overton well south of Wilson's Creek. He tried to remember how the wagon he and Linc Watson had ridden in bounced about, but he gave up when he realized he had come as close to passing out as a man could without actually losing consciousness. He had slept so heavily the bumps and potholes in the road had meant nothing to him, even as the wheel had begun working its way off.

The road turned steep as it wound into a low range of hills that mimicked their larger brothers to the east. The strata showed the distinctly colored bands so common throughout the Badlands. His horse strained to make the grade, forcing Slocum to dismount and walk the gelding up. He had kept the other horse in reserve should he need to make a quick getaway, but the men in Wilson's Creek had discovered a new problem in the night.

He thought the water released from behind the dam had flooded part of the town. All the better to destroy yet another section of Mackenzie's domain.

Slocum huffed and puffed as he hiked uphill, then he slowed and finally stared at the ditch alongside the rocky road. He let out a heartfelt laugh. The wagon would have tipped upward, causing anything in the rear to slide out. He had been asleep and clinging to the side of the wagon. Linc Watson likely had slid out here.

So had the gold dust. Lying in the ditch, half covered with dirt and debris carried by the wind, the bag holding a king's ransom beckoned to him. He brushed it off and tried to lift the bag, only to find he lacked the strength.

Working open the lacing on the top, he peered inside. The familiar smaller leather bags filled it to the brim. Sitting cross-legged, he pulled the leather cord from one and tipped a bit of the gold dust into his palm. The wind whipped it away. It caught on a rising wind current and turned the air golden. He laughed even harder now. He was a rich man, and he had done it at Mackenzie's expense.

Slocum sobered when he realized that wasn't true. This dust had been pulled from the mine by slave labor. Those working to make the mercury-gold amalgam had been driven crazy by the fumes. How many had died for this hundred pounds of gold at his feet could never be told.

He wound the leather strip back around the bag. He would figure out later how to repay those who had survived Mackenzie's predation. First he had to get to Overton. From there a telegram to the army might ensure a troop descending on Wilson's Creek and routing Mackenzie's men.

He considered how best to carry the gold and finally divided the larger bag into two sections, slinging it over the back of his spare horse. The wind spooked the horse and made it difficult for him to secure the bag, even using lengths of rope taken from his lariat.

Then he froze. On the rising wind came a distant sound he thought far behind him. His hand went to his six-shooter as the *whoosh!* of wings drowned out the wind.

A shadow passed over him, then turned to a tiny dot in

the storm-cloudy sky. He went into a crouch, six-gun aimed high at Mackenzie as he banked and came hurtling down like an arrow. Slocum fired twice, missed, fired again. Then his six-shooter came up empty.

He was knocked off his feet as Mackenzie pulled parallel to the ground and thrust out his wings. One tip struck Slocum in the face. Then Mackenzie kicked out and planted a boot in Slocum's belly, knocking him to the ground.

Dazed, Slocum struggled to sit up. Then he cried in pain as talons raked his face. Blood spurted from three shallow grooves slashed across his right cheek. He pressed his hand to the wounds, turned right, and then rolled left as fast as he could to avoid a second deadly strike from the fake thunderbird's talons.

"You ruined my town. You let my slaves go free and you stole my gold! You are going to die for this!" Mackenzie let out a maniacal laugh that chilled Slocum's soul. The words were rational but the sounds escaping along with them were pure loco.

"Sorry I couldn't have done worse to you," Slocum said, scooting along in the dirt. His back pressed against one of the rocks by the road, preventing further retreat.

Mackenzie stalked toward him. The wings snapped back, letting him use his arms freed from the rod and cloth constraints. The sharpened talons glinted in the faint light filtering past the storm clouds. The iron claws flashed when lightning lit the sky. Mackenzie advanced with a curious sliding motion. Slocum saw why. He had fastened talons to his boots, too. What parts of the man that weren't covered with glued-on feathers were deadly with the knife-sharp spikes.

Raking the air back and forth, Mackenzie came closer to Slocum. All he needed was a single hard lunge to impale his victim. Or he could let Slocum bleed to death from dozens of smaller cuts inflicted by the honed edges.

"You will suffer, then I will kill you." Mackenzie kicked

out and caught Slocum in the leg with a spike mounted on his toe. Slocum's leg gave way. He collapsed to the ground.

"I'd like to make you suffer, too, you son of a bitch, but I'll settle for killing your sorry ass!"

Slocum looked past a startled Mackenzie at Erika, aiming a rifle at the man who had held her captive.

"You cannot kill the thunderbird!" Mackenzie cawed like a bird and lunged at her as she pulled the trigger.

Even over the wind, the sound of the hammer falling on a punk cartridge echoed in Slocum's ears. Before Erika could lever in another round, Mackenzie was on her, forcing her to the ground and raising his hand for the killing stroke.

Ignoring the pain in his leg and the cuts on his face, Slocum launched himself through the air and tackled Mackenzie. The two went down in a welter of arms and talons with gaudy feathers flying in all directions, carried away by the storm winds. Slocum held Mackenzie close as they rolled over and over, going down the steep road. To release him now meant instant death. As it was, Mackenzie forced a talon into Slocum's side and sent new waves of pain into his ribs.

Slocum knew what had to be done to stay alive. He had to kill Mackenzie. But he had been battered and beaten and torn up so much that his strength failed him when he needed it most. Worse, Mackenzie's phenomenal upper body strength seemed undiminished. Mackenzie kicked him with a spiked boot and penetrated the leather just above his ankle. Slocum toppled as if a lumberjack had chopped down a tree.

Mackenzie towered above him, lines of madness and anger etching his face. He raised his powerful arms, the talons ready for a killing blow. From higher on the hill Erika cried out. Slocum looked to her, wanting to see her rather than his own death in his last instant.

He blinked and tried to make out what perched on the tall rock beside the road, back where he had found the gold. A screech more terrifying than anything he had ever heard in his life cut through the wind as immense wings spread. The creature dove straight down—heading for Mackenzie.

The madman half turned, saw the approaching juggernaut, and tried to fend it off with his talons. Legs with claws more potent than the puny ones Mackenzie wore cut into his body. Wings flapped powerfully, taking him off his feet. In seconds, his death screams vanished into the wind and thunder. A powerful lightning bolt lit up the sky for an instant, illuminating a gigantic bird with a lifeless body dangling from its claws as it flew away.

Then a sheet of rain marching from the mountains across the road hid the rest of the world.

"John, are you alive?"

"Still kicking," he told Erika. "You showed up at just the right time."

"You're not getting rid of me so easily. I told you I'd wait—and that I'd find you somewhere along the Overton road."

She helped him stand. He needed her support more than he cared to admit. She looked at him, eyes wide with fear. "Did you see that?"

"I didn't see a damned thing," he said. "Let's take the gold, get to Overton, and hole up for a week in a hotel."

"Only a week?" she asked, a faint smile turning up the corners of her mouth.

"Maybe two," he said. "If they have room service."

Supporting each other, they found their horses and rode through the storm, never thinking to find shelter, because they both wanted to put as many miles as possible between themselves and the real thunderbird.

Watch for

SLOCUM AND THE LONG RIDE

417th novel in the exciting SLOCUM series
from Jove

Coming in November!